Noah rested a hand at the small of her back. "Why don't you go sit down. Tell me what you want."

"Oh, you're going to serve me?"

He smiled. "Of course. We Wainwright men may not be able to cook well, but we do know how to serve a woman."

Viviana wanted to remind Noah that she wasn't his woman or even a Wainwright woman but decided to play along. It was better than trading barbs with him. She executed a graceful curtsy. "I'm sorry I barked at you yesterday, and I want to—"

Noah placed a finger over her parted lips, cutting off her apology. His mouth was a hairbreadth from hers. "No apologies. It's in the past, and I don't believe in reliving the past," he said, winking at her. His eyebrows lifted questioningly. "Agree?"

Viviana was too stunned to speak and nodded instead. Noah hadn't kissed her, but that did not stop her heart from beating faster than normal. Did he not know he was much too virile for her to ignore? All he had to do was stare at her, and she felt things she did not want to feel. The scars from her last relationship were still healing, and she did not want to reopen them.

* * *

WICKHAM FALLS WEDDINGS:
Small-town heroes, bighearted love!

Dear Reader,

The Wainwrights are back!

This time it's Noah Wainwright who will take center stage in the latest Wickham Falls Wedding story. I'd asked myself from the first time I introduced Noah to readers in *Because of You* if there was a woman out there who could make him turn in his bachelor card.

Noah decided to answer that question for me when he first met Viviana Remington in *Twins for the Soldier*. Noah is not only smitten with the dark-haired beauty but is totally unaware that the owner of Wickham Falls Bed and Breakfast has just earned her third strike in the game of romance and is also totally immune to his practiced charm. What's a man to do? Noah chooses to let events unfold naturally but never could he have predicted a deal he has executed countless times would not go as planned.

Viviana Remington breaks her vow never to get involved with another man, but she needs hunky blond Noah to save her bed and breakfast. They combine business with pleasure as he takes her on a whirlwind journey of glamorous parties in exotic locales, and when he introduces the small-town girl to his wealthy New York City real-estate family, she knows she's in too deep. But in a single act, Noah will go from dealmaker to heartbreaker and he is forced to choose between the woman he loves and his family.

Y'all come on back to Wickham Falls to discover whether Noah and Viviana can seal the important deal of their lives that promises forever.

Happy reading!

Rochelle Alers

Dealmaker, Heartbreaker

Rochelle Alers

HARLEQUIN SPECIAL EDITION

Recycling programs
for this product may
not exist in your area.

ISBN-13: 978-1-335-57387-2

Dealmaker, Heartbreaker

Copyright © 2019 by Rochelle Alers

www.Harlequin.com

Printed in U.S.A.

Since 1988, national bestselling author **Rochelle Alers** has written more than eighty books and short stories. She has earned numerous honors, including the Zora Neale Hurston Award, the Vivian Stephens Award for Excellence in Romance Writing and a Career Achievement Award from *RT Book Reviews*. She is a member of Zeta Phi Beta Sorority, Inc., Iota Theta Zeta Chapter. A full-time writer, she lives in a charming hamlet on Long Island. Rochelle can be contacted through her website, www.rochellealers.org.

Books by Rochelle Alers

Harlequin Special Edition

Wickham Falls Weddings

Home to Wickham Falls
Her Wickham Falls SEAL
The Sheriff of Wickham Falls

American Heroes

Claiming the Captain's Baby
Twins for the Soldier

Harlequin Kimani Romance

The Eatons

Sweet Silver Bells
Sweet Southern Nights
Sweet Destiny
Sweet Persuasions
Twice the Temptation

Visit the Author Profile page at Harlequin.com for more titles.

Prologue

"How long have the Wolfes owned this property?"

Viviana Remington looked straight ahead rather than glance up at the tall, blond man walking a little too close for her to feel comfortable around him. When she and her brother had decided to sell off eight of twelve undeveloped acres of land on which their ancestral home sat, Giles Wainwright had suggested his developer cousin just might be interested.

However, when Noah Wainwright walked through the doors of The Falls House and stared rudely at her with his large aquamarine eyes, she'd suddenly felt like a specimen on a slide under a microscope. And he had continued to watch her when sharing a light repast with her brother, future sister-in-law and Giles.

Viviana concentrated, carefully putting one booted

foot in front of the other as she led Noah down the sloping footpath into a valley. It had rained heavily the night before, and the earth was still soaked. She chanced a quick glance at him and would've lost her footing if Noah hadn't caught her arm and steadied her. Viviana shivered, not from fear of falling but from the warmth of his hand and the sensual scent of his cologne. After her last disastrous relationship, she did not want a man to touch, look at or even smile at her. She was just that turned off by the opposite sex. And she did not know why, but there was something about Noah that intrigued her, even though she had a preference for dark-haired men.

This time Viviana did give him a direct stare. She wasn't into stereotypes, but Noah did not look like any developer she'd ever seen. She thought he was the perfect prototype for the quintessential California surfer with his long, sun-bleached and shaggy hair falling around his tanned face and neck.

She felt the runaway beating of her heart against her ribs when he moved even closer. "Thank you." The two words were a breathless whisper.

Noah released her arm. "You're quite welcome. But you didn't answer my question."

Suddenly she recalled what he'd asked her. "One hundred fifty years."

Noah whistled softly. "That's a long time. And you want to sell eight acres of your legacy."

"Yes."

"Why?" Noah asked.

"I need the money to make repairs to the main house

and update the guesthouses before I reopen the board-inghouse as a bed-and-breakfast."

Noah stopped and shielded his eyes from the brilliant summer sun as he stared at the verdant landscape with towering trees and wildflowers growing in abandon. This was his second trip to Wickham Falls, a town boasting a population of four thousand permanent residents, and although he found it aesthetically beautiful, it still was much too rural and isolated for his tastes.

"I suppose that's as good excuse as any to sell off land."

"It's not an excuse," Viviana countered, "but a reason."

Lowering his hand, he met her eyes. There was something so incredibly sensual about Viviana Remington that Noah found it difficult to draw a normal breath. He knew it was rude to stare, but sitting across from her at the table, he hadn't been able to pull his eyes away from her black, curly hair framing her delicate face and cascading down her back, her flawless golden-brown complexion, her large and clear toffee-colored eyes, and her full, lush mouth.

A hint of a smile parted his lips. "Are you willing to sell some of your remaining four acres?"

Viviana shook her head. "No. The Falls House sits on two acres, the guesthouses on one, and I need the remaining acre in the event a guest would like to book an outdoor event."

Noah thought about her brother's fiancée's suggestion he either build eight middle-income homes or sixteen moderately priced homes on one or half-acre lots. "I like what I see, but it's going take some time before I decide which type of structures to design." Since joining family-owned-and-operated Wainwright Developers Group, he had become involved in the division responsible for domestic sales.

"You're going to design the homes?"

Noah looked at Viviana as if she had spoken a foreign language. "Yes. Why?"

"I…I thought your focus was being a developer."

His eyebrows lifted slightly. "I'm an architect *and* a developer. Once I get back to New York I'll scan a copy of my degree and send it to you."

She narrowed her eyes at him. "Don't be facetious, Noah. It's not very becoming."

His expression was the epitome of innocence. "I wasn't being facetious, Viviana. I just want to prove that I'm not a fraud."

"Did I say you were a fraud?"

Noah did not want to get into a debate with Viviana about his professional credentials. All he wanted was a verbal agreement as to the price of the land so he could set up in Washington, DC. Whenever he oversaw a new construction project, he'd made it a practice to live close to the site until it was completed.

"How much do you want for the land?"

Viviana crossed her arms under her breasts. "You'll have to discuss that with Leland. He oversees the finances, while I'm responsible for running the business."

"If that's the case, then I suggest we walk back to the house."

Viviana turned on her heel and headed in the direction of the antebellum mansion that showed obvious signs of disrepair. Noah was several steps behind her, which gave him the advantage of watching the fluid sway of her hips in a pair of stretch slacks. She was average height for a woman, slim, but not so slim she would be deemed skinny.

When he had asked his CEO father for authorization to purchase the land, Edward Wainwright had balked at the idea of building in rural West Virginia until Noah reminded him that his nephew Giles lived in Wickham Falls. Edward called him twenty-four hours later and gave his approval.

Noah wiped his boots on the thick mat outside the door and walked into the historic mansion boasting ten bedroom suites to discuss the terms of the sale with Leland Remington.

Chapter One

Three months later...

Noah downshifted and maneuvered onto the road leading to the Wickham Falls Bed and Breakfast. He'd completed the renderings for the homes, surrounded by age-old trees that he planned to build in the valley. The drawings included the retention of much of the natural plant life to blend harmoniously with the existing landscape.

He'd managed to keep busy since his last trip to the coal-mining region with a project in DC. It was the first time WDG had put up luxury condos in the capital city, and most of the units in the twelve-story high-rise were sold before completion. It had taken supreme willpower for Noah not to take a side trip to

Wickham Falls with the hope that he would run into Viviana. There was something about her that made him less confident than he normally was around women. Even though he'd wanted to ask Giles about her, he'd decided it was best he not let his cousin know that his interest in Viviana Remington went beyond business.

Noah was definitely not a novice when it came to interacting with women.

Whether subtle or bold, he knew with a single glance whether or not to approach a woman to let her know that he was interested in her, but that hadn't happened with Viviana. She'd met his eyes and then ignored him as if he did not exist. To say she had deflated his confidence was an understatement.

He had been tempted to ask Giles's wife, Mya, about Viviana because she had grown up in Wickham Falls but then changed his mind once he realized he would have to return to wait for the town board to approve his building application. And when he'd informed Giles that he was coming to Wickham Falls for an extended stay, Giles had invited him to stay with him, his wife and toddler daughter, but Noah declined the invitation, preferring instead to live at the bed-and-breakfast to get to know Viviana better.

Again, Noah was overwhelmed with the natural splendor of the Mountain State. There were tree-covered mountains, lush valleys waterfalls, as well as rapids, lakes, rivers and primordial forest, which was nirvana for hunters and fishermen. He didn't hunt, but he did fish. There was nothing more exciting to Noah than fishing off the side of a boat and catching dinner.

Viviana had said she'd needed to sell the land to make repairs to her home, and as Noah drove up the path leading to the magnificent mansion, his practiced eye immediately saw the changes. The house sported a new coat of paint; the black shutters framing tall energy-saving windows were also new. When he'd first come to the home that the locals called The Falls House, he recognized the design was modeled on architecture found in Barbados. He'd seen many island antebellum homes that were built on raised basements to catch the breeze, but it was odd to see the style in West Virginia where heat and humidity did not equal those areas farther south.

He slowed to less than five miles an hour when he saw a tall, slender man with a long, snow-white ponytail come out of the house with Viviana. With wide eyes, Noah stared at her as she embraced the man before he got into a late-model, gray pickup and started the engine. Maneuvering over to the side of the road, he let the man drive past him. Their eyes had met for a millisecond, yet it was long enough for Noah to surmise he was Viviana's father. There was something about the man's features that called to mind her brother Leland.

Viviana smiled when she saw Noah emerge from the racy silver sports car with New York plates. Her first impression of him having looked like a surfer was shattered completely with his transformation. The blond hair was fashionably barbered with a side part and heavy waves brushed off his forehead. She knew in a single glance that his charcoal-gray slacks had not come off a rack and his stark white shirt with a mono-gram on the left French cuff was also custom-made.

She had recommended Noah talk to her brother about how much he wanted for the sale of the land, and once Leland disclosed the amount Viviana hadn't been able to say anything for several minutes. The Wainwright Developers Group had paid them more than three times the prevailing rate for land in a region where many people lived at or below the poverty line. Leland did not disclose the details of the negotiations between him, Giles, and Noah, and told her to use the money to make repairs and upgrade the house.

She smiled and extended her hand with Noah's approach. He had called her the day before to inform her he had finished the blueprints for the homes he planned to build in the valley and would stay until the town council approved his prospectus.

"Welcome back to The Falls."

Ignoring the proffered hand, Noah leaned over and kissed her cheek. "Thank you."

Viviana's eyes caressed his face, finding him even more attractive than when she'd first seen him. She normally didn't attribute the word *beautiful* to a man, but Noah was just that. "If you'd come earlier I would have introduced you to my father."

Noah's eyes caressed her face. "Is he coming back?"

"No. He just drove down from Philadelphia to spend a few days with me. My father is a professional artist who has just been commissioned to paint a mural for the lobby of a major bank's headquarters."

"That's impressive."

She smiled. "I agree. As an architect I'm certain the two of you would've had a lot talk about when it comes to shapes and colors." Mya Wainwright had disclosed, during Noah's visit, that he was an architect and her husband an engineer and that they talked incessantly about buying, selling, designing and erecting buildings. "Please come in, and I'll show you to the suite I've assigned to you."

Noah hesitated. "If it's all right with you, I'd rather stay in one of the guesthouses. I need the privacy to conduct business with my home office and potential clients. Will that be a problem?" he added when her jaw dropped.

"Oh no," Viviana said quickly. When Noah alerted her about his arrival, she'd assigned him the largest suite of the five she had set aside for guests. "I have a vacancy in the second guesthouse. A writer, who insists on anonymity and is only known by his popular pseudonym, has taken up residence in the first one for the next two months while he claims he's writing the sequel to one of his blockbuster novels."

"If I don't recognize him, then I don't need to know who he is."

Viviana nodded. Her reclusive guest had paid for the guesthouse two months in advance. He allowed housekeeping to come in to clean only twice a week while he went for a walk to gather his thoughts. Viviana thought it weird that he only ate freeze-dried prepackaged meals people purchased in the event of a catastrophic event that would destroy the country's food supply. But, it did not matter how eccentric he was as long as he did not burn down the guesthouse.

"Come on in. I have to get your key card. It's too late for breakfast, but if you want I can fix something for you to eat," Viviana said over her shoulder as Noah followed her into the great room.

"Please don't bother. I told Giles I would hang out with him and Mya later this afternoon. I'll probably have dinner with them."

"The last time I saw Lily she was talking up a storm."

"That's because she's a Wainwright. When everyone gets together, if you don't talk fast you won't get a word in edgewise."

Viviana walked into the room next to the parlor that she had set up as her office. She swiped a key card over the sensor and pushed open the door. The room was off-limits to everyone in the ten-bedroom house. Since the bed-and-breakfast had opened for business, she had hired a part-time cook, two part-time housekeepers and a landscape company to maintain the grounds.

She opened a desk drawer and removed two key cards and activated them. "I'm giving you two in case you misplace one."

Noah took the cards and handed her a credit card. "I don't know how long I'm staying, but put all of the charges on this card."

Viviana stared at the black card as if it was a venomous snake. She shook her head. "I'm not going to take that."

"Why not?"

She glared at him. "Because I'm not going to take any more money from you, that's why."

Noah's eyes flashed with glints of anger. "You're right when you say that your brother handles the finances. How do expect to run a viable business when you let folks lay up for free?"

Viviana felt as if he'd given her a stinging slap across the face as she recoiled from his acerbic taunt. She closed her eyes and counted slowly until she felt her anger subside and could say what was on her mind without regretting what she actually wanted to tell him.

"When I told you to talk to Leland about buying the land, I didn't think you would pay us more than the prevailing rate for land around here, and that means I'm not going to take advantage of you. Now that you own my land I consider you a business partner, and that means extending certain privileges. You can stay in the guesthouse without me charging you, or you can go and live with your cousin. If you decide not to stay, then give me the key cards and get back in your fancy little sports car and drive away."

Noah looked at Viviana as if she had taken leave of her senses, and he wanted to tell her he wasn't her ex looking to fleece her. The rise and fall of her breasts under a white blouse and the slight flaring of her delicate nostrils told him she wasn't just annoyed but angry. All he wanted to do was pay her for living in the guesthouse, and she'd gone off on him.

At that point he did not want to do or say anything that would drive a wedge between them. It was apparent he had underestimated Viviana. She had come at him like a cat he'd once seen that'd had a litter of kittens. The one time he tried picking up one of the kittens, the queen sprang and dug her claws into the back of his hand until he let go of her baby.

"Okay, you win," he said after an uneasy silence.

"It's not about winning and losing," Viviana retorted. "It's about what is right and wrong."

Noah threw up a hand in exasperation. "You're right, Viviana."

"Please don't attempt to placate me."

Noah smothered a savage expletive under his breath as he forced a smile. "I'm sorry. I think I can find the guesthouse without your assistance." At that point he did not care if she felt he was being facetious. All he wanted to do was get away from Viviana before he said something he would come to regret.

He walked out of the house, got into his car and drove around to the guesthouses. As he unloaded the trunk of luggage and electronic equipment, Noah thought about Viviana's attitude toward him during their first encounter. At that time, he hadn't known what had made her unapproachable, but now he knew it had something to do with a man—a man who'd used her and nearly ruined her financially. What she would soon learn, however, was that he did not take advantage of women.

He'd sown his wild oats, and now at thirty-three, he was looking forward to finding that special woman with whom to settle down. Some of his friends teased him, saying he was still too young to talk about marrying and having kids, but few knew that Noah had tired of the nonstop, never-ending parties where he woke feeling worse than when he'd gone to sleep, that he'd dated too many girls. However, he had always been very discriminating when sleeping with a woman. He really had to like and date a woman to make love with her. And when he looked back at his continual party days, he was proud to admit he hadn't used women.

He swiped the key card, and the door opened. The lingering distinctive smell of lemon wafted to his nostrils. Noah discovered the structure contained two bedrooms, and there was a loft with a king-size bed overlooking the living/dining area. The kitchen and bath were updated, and the furniture contemporary and functional. A desk, worktable and chair were set up in a corner under a window which was the perfect spot for him to conduct business.

Noah picked up a brochure on the desk advertising the amenities the bed-and-breakfast offered. There was a buffet breakfast for guests from seven to ten. Check out was at 11:00 a.m., and early check-in was at 2:00 p.m. Cordials and sweet breads were served in the parlor at 8:00 p.m., and all rooms were wired with free cable and Wi-Fi.

He decided to unpack, shower and change his clothes, then drive over to see his cousin. Perhaps Giles could give him a better read on the enigmatic, beautiful woman with whom he had found himself enthralled.

Chapter Two

Noah stood in the middle of the kitchen, smiling when he saw Giles kiss his wife's forehead. His cousin had changed since becoming a husband and father. And now that Mya had recently announced she was pregnant with their second child, Giles had begun complaining about traveling and leaving her and Lily behind.

"Noah and I are going to sit out on the porch for a while. I promise not to take too long."

Mya smiled at her husband, her hazel eyes softening. "Take your time. I know you and Noah have a lot to talk about. I'll probably be asleep when you come up."

Noah wanted to tell Mya it wasn't business he wanted to discuss with her husband, but Viviana. "I promise not to keep him too long."

He sat on a rocker facing Giles and stared out at the darkening sky. The air in the mountains was cool and crisp. "I can see why you live here. Everything is so quiet and peaceful."

Giles's teeth shone brightly in his face, darkened by the hot Bahamian sun. "Am I hearing you right, little coz? The last time you were here, you complained that it was too quiet, that you could hear crickets in the daytime."

"You're right about that," Noah agreed. "There's something about living in the mountains that makes you think and feel differently. But that doesn't mean I'm ready to move here."

"Does that difference have anything to do with a beautiful young woman with long black hair?"

Noah looked directly at his cousin. "What are you talking about?"

"Not *what* but *who*, Noah. You think everyone didn't notice you gawking at Viviana Remington like a lovesick puppy the first time you met her?"

"That's because she is beautiful."

"I'm not saying she isn't, Noah. I try not to listen to gossip, but I overheard Mya talking about Viviana breaking up with her boyfriend. I don't know and don't want to know what happened between them, but right about now she wants nothing to do with men."

Noah shifted on the cushioned rocker. "He stole her identity."

Giles sat straight. "Damn! No wonder she doesn't trust men." He paused. "But she wouldn't have to worry about that with you because you don't need her money.

By the way, did you know that you offered to pay her and her brother a lot more than that land is worth?"

He knew Giles was privy to the payout because every Wainwright was given a monthly report of every purchase and sale. "You noticed that?"

"Yeah, I did, but I decided to defend the expenditure because otherwise your daddy would've raised holy hell. The older Uncle Teddy gets the more he tries to pinch pennies."

Noah smiled. "Thanks for covering my ass." He'd driven up to New York for the monthly board meeting, and when the subject of the purchase of land in West Virginia had been brought up, it was Giles and not Noah who had defended the decision to buy the parcels.

"I did it in the name of love. Now, what are you going to do with Viviana? Should I assume she's not falling for your so-called million-dollar charm?"

"I'm not trying to charm her, Giles. I know when a woman doesn't want anything to do with me. But on the other hand, I've spent the past three months thinking about her. I don't know what it is, but I can't get her out of my head."

"Have you been seeing someone else in the meantime?"

"No. And I don't want to."

"The only thing I'm going to say is not to put any pressure on her. It's best that you become friends before you think about sleeping with the woman."

"That's not even a thought at this time."

"Good. Then take it slow, coz. How long do you plan to hang out here?"

Noah lifted his shoulders. "I don't know. Tomorrow I'm going to the town hall to register my name for the zoning-board meeting to submit my proposal. Then I have to wait for a hearing."

"What else do you have on your calendar?"

Noah shook his head. "Nothing but time. After the DC project I decided to take a break. I've been going nonstop for more than a year, and it's time I get off the real-estate roller coaster."

Giles exhaled an audible breath. "I hear you. I'm definitely going to slow down once Mya has this baby. It's time your brother Rhett dips his toe in this crazy business."

"Rhett is too much like Jordan. They love the law."

"If not Rhett, then Chanel. She's graduated college with a degree in business and finance. It's time we have a woman sitting at the table."

"She would be the first one," Noah confirmed.

"If you agree with me, then when we have the next board meeting I'm going to bring it up," Giles said.

"It will probably bring holy hell down on you from some of the other family members, but don't worry because I'll have your back."

Giles smiled. "That's all I need because you're the only one who has been able to go a couple of rounds with your father and our grandfather and come out winning most of the time."

"That's only because I refuse to be intimidated. My father just got hard once he took over the company, but it's Grandpa who is the pit bull. That old gangster still has a gun in his desk drawer."

"That's because he is a gangster down to the marrow in his bones," Giles joked.

Noah laughed. He'd heard rumors that his grandfather had been a teenage bagman for criminals who controlled the illegal numbers on the Lower East Side. He sobered. "I'm going to take your advice about taking it slow with Viviana. I'll give her all of the time she needs to come to the realization that I don't want to take advantage of her."

"The only other thing I'm going to say is not to hurt her emotionally or you'll have to answer to her brother. The man is an ex–Army Ranger, and those Special Forces dudes are crazy."

"I don't plan to hurt her, Giles."

"I'm not saying you would, but just keep it in mind if things don't work out."

Noah stood up and stretched his arms over his head. He was tired from the long drive from New York to West Virginia, and right now all he craved was a bed. "I'm leaving. Kiss Mya and Lily for me."

Giles got up. "I will."

"Do you have any plans to fly down to the Bahamas?"

"No. I told my father I'm taking a break until Mya completes her first trimester."

Noah patted his older cousin's back. "Good for you. Thanks for dinner and the talk."

Giles hugged his cousin. "Anytime, coz."

Noah folded his tall frame into the low-slung Porsche and fastened the seat belt. Tapping a button, he brought the powerful engine roaring to life, and he executed a perfect U-turn and headed back in the opposite direction.

There was only one car in the section designated for guest parking when he drove past the main house, and he wondered if Viviana had enough guests to sustain the bed-and-breakfast. He parked his car behind the guesthouse and walked around to open the front door. He lingered long enough to brush his teeth before climbing into bed. An audible sigh echoed in the bedroom decorated in monochromatic hues of blues when he pulled a lightweight blanket over his nude body. Within minutes he fell asleep, and for the first time in a very long time, he wasn't disturbed by erotic dreams of making love to a faceless woman he knew was Viviana.

Viviana had just finished inspecting the dishes the cook had set over warmers on the buffet server when Noah walked into the dining room. She smiled, and she wasn't disappointed when he returned it with a friendly one. After he'd left, she'd chided herself for her waspish tone when he had done nothing to deserve it. Viviana knew if she did not stop believing every man was like her con-man ex, then she would never be able to move on with her life. Thankfully, Leland had paid the delinquent property taxes, and with the land sale, she was able to repair and update the property and put some money away for the proverbial rainy day. Now she was ready to reclaim the life she had before her last failed relationship.

Her admiring gaze took in Noah's crisp light blue shirt he had paired with slim-fitting jeans and Doc Martens. "Good morning. Did you sleep well?"

He stared at her under lowered lids. "Like a newborn in his mama's arms."

"Good." She pointed to the buffet table. "Breakfast is ready. Let me know if you want an omelet, and I'll have the cook make one for you."

Noah glanced around the dining room with a table set for six. "How many guests are you expecting?"

"Only two. A couple checked in late last night, and they'll probably be down later."

"Did you eat?"

Viviana shook her head. "I had a cup of coffee. I'll eat later."

"Will it bother you if I ask you to eat with me? I hate eating alone."

She wondered if he was extending an olive branch when it should've been her apologizing for her sharp tongue. "Of course I'll eat with you." She pointed to a round table in the corner with place settings for two. "We can eat over there."

Noah rested a hand at the small of her back. "Why don't you go and sit down. Tell me what you want."

"Oh, you're going to serve me?"

He smiled. "Of course. We Wainwright men may not be able to cook well, but we do know how to serve a woman."

Viviana wanted to remind Noah that she wasn't his woman or even a Wainwright woman but decided to play along. It was better than trading barbs with him. She executed a graceful curtsy. "I'm sorry I barked at you yesterday, and I want to—"

Noah placed a finger over her parted lips, cutting off

her apology. His mouth was a hairbreadth from hers. "No apologies. It's in the past, and I don't believe in reliving the past," he said, winking at her. His eyebrows lifted questioningly. "Agree?"

Viviana was too stunned to speak and nodded instead. Noah hadn't kissed her, but that did not stop her heart from beating faster than normal. Did he not know he was much too virile for her to ignore? All he had to do was stare at her, and she felt things she did not want to feel. The scars from her last relationship were still healing, and she did not want to reopen them.

"What do you want?"

"Bring me whatever you're going to eat."

"What if I bring enough for us to share?" he asked.

Viviana smiled. "Okay."

The cook always prepared enough for the registered guests and staff, eliminating the need for storing leftovers or throwing food away—something she loathed because there were people in The Falls that depended on the church's outreach pantry to supply them with staples they needed to feed their families.

She watched Noah fill several plates and balance them along his arm as he returned to the table, and she wondered if he had been a waiter but quickly dashed the idea because of what she'd gleaned about the Wainwrights. She knew Noah and Giles did not have to wait tables to earn extra pocket money like a lot of young men she knew. Fortunately for her, she and Leland were exempt; they weren't as wealthy as their ancestors, the Johnson County Wolfes, but they had still grown up in relative comfort.

"It looks as if you've had a lot of practice waiting tables," she teased when he set down four dishes with scrambled eggs, home fries, bacon, sausage patties and sliced melon.

Noah winked at her again. "I'm auditioning for a job in your dining room."

Her smile grew wider, bringing his gaze to linger on her lips. "I haven't advertised for a waiter."

Noah tugged on the single braid falling down her back. "If you decide to advertise, then I'm willing to take the position. I'm going back to get some juice and coffee."

Viviana held his arm. "Sit down and eat. I'll get the beverages. What do you want?"

"Cranberry juice and black coffee."

She got up and walked over to the beverage table and filled a glass with chilled juice and a mug with coffee. Noah stood up when she returned to the table and pulled out the chair to seat her. Viviana did not have too many memories of her parents together when she was a young girl, but the one that had lingered was when her father would pull out a chair to seat her mother. It was a habit he had repeated with her whenever they were together.

She smiled at him over her shoulder. "Thank you."

It was several seconds before he returned the smile and nodded.

Noah spread a cloth napkin over his lap and then picked up a forkful of fluffy scrambled eggs. They were delicious. "The cook gets an A."

"I'll let him know."

He took a sip of the hot coffee. "The dishes you and

your sister-in-law made when I first came here were exceptional. Where did you learn to cook like that?"

"My aunt is a professional chef and taught me and my brother. Lee's an excellent cook, but once he graduates culinary school he's going to be exceptional."

"What about your mother? Is she a good cook?"

She stared at her plate. "My mother died when I was seven. Talking about my parents is a long story that I really don't want to get into right now."

Reaching across the table, Noah held her left hand. "I'm sorry, Viviana. You don't ever have to tell me if you don't want to."

Her head popped up. "One of these days, maybe I'll feel comfortable enough with you to tell you the whole sordid story about my family."

His hand tightened on her fingers. "I'm willing to bet my family's secrets are just as sordid or even more so than yours."

Her eyes grew wider. "They couldn't be."

Noah leaned over the table. "Do yours include affairs, secret babies and gangsters?"

Viviana's jaw dropped. "Well…no."

He released her fingers and sat back in his chair. "The only thing I'm going to say is if you have enough money, you can bury your secrets for a while, but then somehow they come to the surface and you'll have to own it." Noah stared over her head. "How many guests are you averaging a week?"

She shrugged her shoulders. "Probably around four. I know it's not much, but I'm counting on more once hunting season begins."

"And how long is that?"

"Two weeks in November. I don't expect to be at full capacity until the spring and summer during tourist season. This is my first time operating a B and B, so next year I'm thinking of closing down from late November to early April."

"Did you operate the boardinghouse year-round?" Noah hoped talking to Viviana about her business instead of herself would allow her to relax enough to feel completely at ease with him.

"Yes. I had regular boarders who paid by the month, and I served them two meals a day—breakfast and dinner. The problem was I had to be available around the clock every day of the year, and that was exhausting even with regular staff."

Noah nodded. "I believe a bed-and-breakfast is less taxing. Once your elusive writer moves out, you should consider renting that guesthouse to a tenant who would be responsible for their own meals and laundry."

"Now you sound like Angela. She wanted me to advertise the guesthouses as rentals, which would bring in steady income."

"You have ten bedroom suites in this house, five in each wing you've designated for business and the other five for personal use. And if you're going to wait for the spring to fill the business suites, then you can't expect much of a profit margin."

"I've factored that into my budget projection. That's why none of my employees are full-timers."

"What about your cook?"

"He comes in at six and leaves at nine. I take over

the kitchen duties and serve guests until ten, and then I clean up the kitchen."

"That's a lot of work."

"I know, but it has to be done, and I'm not too proud to roll up my sleeves and work. Once Lee comes back, it will get easier because he'll take over the kitchen."

"When is he expected back?"

"Not until he and Angela graduate college."

Noah blinked slowly. "And that is?"

"Almost four years from now."

Noah went completely still. He'd thought Viviana was going to say one or two but not four years. "When you had the boardinghouse, did you run it by your-self?"

"Not initially. My aunt cooked while my uncle took care of the repairs and the grounds. I helped out with laundry and cleaning the rooms. But after Aunt Babs and my uncle relocated to Arizona, I was responsi-ble for running the boardinghouse because Lee was in the army. He only came back when I told him that the county had placed a lien on the property for back taxes."

"He was back, and now he's gone."

Viviana narrowed her eyes, again reminding him of a cat ready to strike. "Please don't talk about my brother, Noah. Precisely because I have a knack of at-tracting the wrong men, my brother had to give up a military career to come back and save our home."

"Why are you blaming yourself for a decision he made? He could've taken a leave and then reenlisted before the year was up. I happen to know that much about the military."

"That's what he'd originally planned, but Angela wouldn't have married him because she was a military widow and she did not want to go through that again. She hadn't delivered her twins when her first husband was killed."

Noah slumped in the chair and ran a hand over his face. "Oh, I'm so sorry I said what I said to you about your brother."

"Don't beat up on yourself. You didn't know. I think we should reserve judgment of each other because there is so much I don't know about you and you don't know about me, Noah."

"You're right," he said in agreement.

"Anytime you want to know something about me and my family, all you have to do is ask," he said, smiling.

"Aren't you afraid I'll spill my guts to a tabloid reporter?"

"No. A tabloid tried that before and my grandfather shut them down."

Her mouth formed a perfect O. "My bad."

Throwing back his head, Noah laughed. "And you don't have to worry about me repeating your family gossip," he said once he stopped laughing.

"It doesn't matter because everyone in The Falls knows about the Wolfes and their offspring. There was a time when the Wolfes were like the Bernie Madoffs of Johnson County. They screwed over everyone who came into contact with them." She touched her napkin to the corners of her mouth. "That's something I'll tell you about at another time."

Noah glanced at his watch. "I'm going to leave now

to go over to the town hall to file my application." He rose to stand. "I know you only serve breakfast, but will I see you for dinner?"

"Are you cooking?" Viviana teased.

"I can bring back takeout."

She stood up. "Forget takeout. I'll cook."

Noah stacked the dishes and flatware, carried them to the kitchen and set them in a deep stainless-steel sink filled with soapy water. He'd wanted to tell Viviana that she needed to hire a night manager but knew she probably would resent his interference or believe he thought that because she was a woman she wasn't capable of running her own business. He returned to the guesthouse to get the paperwork he needed to present to the Wickham Falls Zoning Board, which he hoped would go over and approve his prospectus.

As his conversation with a Wickham Falls city clerk ended, Noah felt as if he was in an alternate universe. He couldn't believe what he was hearing. The clerk had examined his documents and then told him he couldn't build residential homes on the property because it had been zoned for commercial use when the Remingtons were approved to convert their personal residence into a boardinghouse. The only way he could erect homes was if Viviana filed to convert her property from commercial to residential, and then he would have to refile for a resident permit. Noah knew he had to disclose the details of his conversation with the clerk to Viviana.

Viviana sat at the desk in her office scrolling through a list of vendors she had to pay when she glanced up to find Noah standing in the doorway. She waved to him. "Come in."

"Only if you're not busy."

"I can do this later." She came around the desk and sat on a tapestry-covered love seat. She patted the cushion beside her. "Come and sit down."

Noah closed the door, sat down and took her hand in his and told her about his visit to the town hall. "You've got to be kidding." A cold shiver had swept over her as if she had been dumped in an ice bath. She did not want to believe that Noah had purchased land on which he couldn't build because it wasn't zoned for residential structures.

He gave her a direct stare. "I wish I was. I was under the assumption that your property is zoned for residential, and if you wanted to operate a business then you would only have to file for a permit and not rezone it for commercial use."

Her eyes filled with unshed tears. "That statute has been on the books for years and is based on the size of the owner's property. Anyone holding more than five acres is required to rezone if they wish to operate a business." She exhaled an audible breath. "I can't pay you back because I've used most of the money to make repairs, and I can't ask Lee for more money because now he has a family to support."

Leaning closer, Noah pressed his thumb to her cheek where a single tear had slipped down her face. "I don't want the money. Perhaps you can file for a waiver."

Her eyelids fluttered. "The zoning board doesn't issue waivers."

Viviana shook her head. "What alternative do we have, Noah?"

"Business is slow right now, so why don't you close for the season and apply for a residential conversion, and once it's approved I can submit my application to build? After I get my approval, you can resubmit for commercial zoning."

She replayed his explanation over in her head several times. Her smile was as bright as the rays of a rising sun. "That's an incredible idea." She leaned over and kissed him, but as she attempted to pull away, Noah released her hand and cupped her face in his palms and deepened the kiss until she swallowed his breath. Her face and her body were on fire. She lowered her eyes demurely. Viviana had not meant to kiss Noah, but the instant his mouth covered hers she did not want to stop. It had been much too long since she had enjoyed the intimacy of the tender gesture. "I'm sorry about that."

Anchoring a hand under her chin, Noah raised her face. "I'm not. I have to confess that I'd wanted to kiss you the day you took me on a tour of the property."

Moisture spiked her lashes as she managed a trembling smile. "Well, you got your wish." Her joy was short-lived as her smile faded when she thought about her employees. "Closing down will cause a cash-flow problem. How am I going to pay my employees? Even though they are seasonal, I'm committed to pay them per diem when necessary."

"Can you apply for a short-term business loan to tie you over?" Noah questioned.

"No. I had to file for bankruptcy, so it's going to be years before I'll be able to reestablish credit."

Noah ran a hand over her hair. "What if I loan you the money to pay your employees, and you can pay me back once the B and B is up and running again. No strings attached."

"I can't, Noah."

His expression changed, becoming a mask of stone. "You can and you will. I've invested too much time and money in this project to piss it away because of a technicality. I'm going to New York next week for my father's sixty-fifth birthday party, but I'll be back to stay until it's time for me to resubmit my application, and hopefully that shouldn't take more than a month."

Viviana bit her lip. "Let me think about it."

"Don't think too long, Viviana. Remember, I work on a timeline when it comes to construction projects."

"I understand."

Noah stood up and walked out, closing the door behind him. Viviana wanted to call Leland and tell him about her dilemma but knew it was time she stopped going to her brother for advice. He'd bailed her out before and had relinquished all financial responsibility for the house and property, and as a businesswoman the final decision would have to come from her.

Chapter Three

Viviana's guests checked out in the early afternoon and by five she had the B and B to herself. She flipped the vacancy sign over to No Vacancy, locked the front door and then walked into her office and flopped down on the love seat, wondering why she had to continue to dodge the slings and arrows of life itself.

She'd been seven when she lost her mother, and even younger when she recalled her father being there and then leaving without saying where he was going or when he was coming back. There was never a time when she could count on him being there for her because he was just that unreliable. Men in her life had become revolving doors, here today and gone tomorrow, leaving a trail of emotional wreckage behind. Viviana knew whenever she'd become involved with a man, she was unconsciously looking for someone to replace her father with, a man she could trust and depend on to protect her when she needed it most. And she wasn't certain whether they innately recognized her vulnerability and took advantage of her willingness to sacrifice her own happiness to make them happy. It had taken her years to realize she gave more in a relationship than she received, and once it ended she not only blamed them but also herself.

The doorbell rang, and she left the love seat to look at the monitor that was programmed to the bell. It was Noah. She'd forgotten they were to eat dinner together. She went to the door and opened it. He was grinning like a Cheshire cat as he raised a large shopping bag in his right hand.

"What did you bring?"

"Dinner."

Viviana opened the door wider. "You didn't have to bring takeout."

Noah stepped into the entryway. "Did you cook?"

"No. Not yet."

"That's why I decided to bring dinner." He lowered his head and kissed her cheek. "Please let me in and close the door before someone drives by and decides to stop. Tonight I want you all to myself so we can talk over a few things without being interrupted."

She closed the door and pressed her back against it. "What things, Noah?"

He leaned closer, his warm, moist breath feathering over her mouth. "Us. You and me, Viviana."

"What about us?"

"We're going to have to figure out a way to work together without sniping at each other."

She angled her head in an attempt to read his closed expression in the muted illumination from the entryway's hanging fixture. "Is that what you think we do? *Snipe?*"

Noah cupped her elbow and eased her away from the door. "Let's go into the kitchen so we can talk and eat." When she did not move, he said, "Please, sweetheart."

Viviana stared up at him through her lashes, unaware of the gesture's seductiveness. "Do you call all women *sweetheart*?"

"No. Just the ones I really like."

"My, my, my. Aren't you the silver-tongued devil," she teased.

Noah chuckled. "One of these days, you'll come to realize that I never say anything I don't mean."

Viviana led the way to the kitchen. "Are you saying you never lie?"

"I can't say never. I grew up with my parents warning me to never lie to them. They wanted me to tell the truth, even if it was something that would break their hearts."

She flipped the light switch, and recessed lights and pendants illuminated the enormous space. "Did you ever break their hearts?"

Noah set the bag on the countertop. "Once."

Viviana met his luminous blue-green eyes. "Is it too personal to disclose?" Now that they'd shared a kiss she felt comfortable asking him about his private life.

"Nah. I was sixteen when my friend raided his family's liquor cabinet, and we drank from every open bottle of gin, scotch, whiskey and brandy to see which tasted best. To say I was sick was an understatement," Noah continued as he removed containers of food from the shopping bag. "I managed to make it home where I gargled with mouthwash and got into bed before I collapsed. My mother came looking for me when I didn't show up for dinner. I lied and told her I wasn't feeling well but didn't tell her why."

"She believed you."

Noah nodded. "Initially she did. The first time I threw up she suspected food poisoning, but none of the kids at my school were experiencing the same symptoms. What I didn't know at the time was that my friend had been drinking for years, so he wasn't hungover. My mother called the doctor, and when I threw up again, he told her he could smell alcohol, and that's when I realized I'd been found out."

"She grounded you."

"How did you know?"

"Because that's what I would've done if my son or daughter were engaged in underage drinking." Although Noah's parents grounded him it hadn't been the same with her because she hadn't had her mother or father as a family unit when growing up, and for that she envied him. She loved her aunt and uncle but they could not replace her parents.

Viviana reached into an overhead cabinet and took down several plates. "Should I assume you learned your lesson about not telling the truth?"

Noah nodded. "Big-time."

"Do you want to eat here or in the dining room?"

Noah glanced around the yawning space that reminded him of one of the two kitchens at the Fifth Avenue mansion where he'd grown up.

"I'd like to eat here." The kitchen was his favorite room in a house. Although he couldn't cook, he loved watching the prep work and enjoyed the different mouthwatering aromas when the chef opened the oven doors.

"I see you discovered Ruthie's."

Noah nodded. "I called Giles, and he told me Ruthie's is best for family eating and the Wolfe Den offers some of the best barbecue in the county, but I'd have to get there early because they usually sell out before closing. I find it odd there's no fast-food restaurants around here."

Viviana set a round table with seating for four with glasses, plates, flatware, and serving bowls and dishes. She removed a pitcher of lemonade from the refrigerator and filled the tall glasses.

"That's because we don't want or need fast-food joints, because it would impact on the viability of Ruthie's and the Den. If you hang out here long enough, you'll discover folks in The Falls like their mom-and-pop shops and want nothing to do with big-box stores or fast-food restaurants. They are wary of outsiders looking to squeeze out the little guy with the guise that they can offer you more variety."

Noah stared at her. "Are you hinting that I shouldn't build small homes that resemble mega mansions?"

She gave him a sidelong glance. "I hope that's not a dig at this house."

"No. It has nothing to do with a house that was built

more than hundred years ago. After we finish eating, I'll show you the renderings of what I've designed."

"How many do you have?"

"Three."

"Why so many?" she asked.

"Once I have a surveyor map out the land, I'll know which one I'll use."

Viviana emptied a container of steaming collard greens into a bowl. "Are the greens for me or both of us?"

Noah winked at her. "Both of us, of course."

"So, the New York City boy likes soul food."

He smiled. "Don't hate, Viv. I've just spent the last five months in and out of DC overseeing the construction of condos, and not only did I develop a taste for collard greens but also biscuits, cornbread, black-eyed peas and chitterlings."

Viviana wrinkled her nose. "I agreed with everything you ate until you said *chitlins*."

"Isn't it *chitterlings*?"

"Nah. Down here we drop the *g*, so it's *chitlins*."

Noah smiled. "I have to remember that the next time I order them. Do you know how to cook them?"

"No because I can't get past the smell of hog intestines. My aunt used to put them in a bucket of vinegar and leave it outside the house for a couple of days before cleaning them. I must admit they did smell good when cooking, but I still refused to eat them."

"Did your aunt learn to cook chitlins at Johnson and Wales University's culinary arts program in Charlotte, North Carolina?"

Viviana dropped a serving spoon, the sound making a dull thud on the cloth-covered mahogany table. "How did you know she attended that college?"

Rounding the table, Noah pulled out a chair for her. "Please sit down, and I'll tell you everything while we eat." He knew it was time he level with Viviana if he hoped to have a relationship with her and prayed what he was about to tell her wouldn't make that impossible. He sat opposite Viviana, his eyes fixed on her delicate features. "Once I decided to offer to purchase your land, I had someone investigate you and your family, but unfortunately the investigator did not look into the zoning laws. Apparently he dropped the ball once it was verified that you and your brother owned the property and felt he didn't need to delve beyond that." He held up a hand when she opened her mouth. "Please let me finish, Viviana.

"It's a company policy that was instituted by my grandfather after he was scammed out of hundreds of thousands of dollars by an unscrupulous client who'd sold him properties he didn't own."

Viviana took a swallow of lemonade, staring at Noah over the rim of the glass. "What about me, Noah? How much do you know about me?"

Noah resisted the urge to round the table and pull Viviana into his arms when he saw anguish in the large light brown eyes with the darker centers. "You already told me about the con man who scammed you out of everything that forced you to file for bankruptcy."

"And you know all of this and you still wanted to go through with the sale?"

"Yes, Viv. I felt as if you and your brother had gone through enough, and that's why I decided to sign off on the sale."

"Did you use any of your own money?"

He glanced down at his plate. "Some of it."

"Why, Noah? Why would you do that knowing that I was forced to file for bankruptcy?"

He rested an elbow on the table. "Do you really have to ask me that?"

"But I am asking, Noah."

Noah exhaled audibly. He'd told Viviana about what the investigator had uncovered, and now it was time for him to tell her the truth. "Because I like you."

"That's not a very good reason," she countered, "and please don't pity me."

A wry smile twisted his mouth. "It's a good enough reason for me, and the last thing I want to do is pity you. You have to be an unbelievably strong woman to have gone through losing your mother at seven, and being seen as an easy mark by a man and still be standing. After graduating college, I refused to join the family company and embarked on a somewhat hedonistic journey that included nonstop parties that went on for days. I didn't do drugs, and I was careful not to overindulge in alcohol because I didn't want a repeat of the episode when we'd raided the liquor cabinet, but I did do a few things that I'm not particularly proud of."

"What about women, Noah?"

His eyebrows lifted. "What about them?"

"Did you sleep with a lot of them?"

He shook his head. "Not so many I can't remember their names."

Viviana picked up a forkful of collards. "Are you telling me this because you want to buy my affection?"

"I didn't have to say anything to you about what I know, and it still wouldn't have made a difference. I'm man enough to let you know that I like you the way a man likes a woman, and it has nothing to do with our deal."

"And if I agree to accept your loan, I hope you don't expect me to sleep with you."

Noah did not want to believe Viviana thought he would put pressure on her to sleep with him because he'd offered to cover the cost of paying her employees until the B and B reopened. "No, Viv, I don't expect you to sleep with me. And to prove that to you, I'd like you to be my plus-one at my friend's destination wedding in the Bahamas over the Veterans Day weekend. I'll reserve a villa with connecting suites."

Viviana wanted to laugh, but what Noah had proposed wasn't exactly funny. They'd had two encounters three months ago, and this was their second encounter since he'd returned to The Falls, and now he'd invited her to travel out of the country with him.

She leaned over the table. "Are you attempting to blackmail me?"

"Of course not," Noah said quickly.

"Well, it sounds like blackmail to me, Noah. You offer to cover my business expenses until I reopen the B and B with the proviso I leave the country with you.

We may have a business arrangement, but I refuse to be used as a pawn for your benefit."

Noah lowered his eyes. "I'm sorry, Viviana. I don't want you to think I'm attempting to take advantage of you."

"But you are," she argued softly.

Noah exhaled an audible sigh. "I sorry you feel this way."

"So am I," Viviana retorted. "Don't you have a girl-friend you'd like to take instead of me?"

"No, because I don't have a girlfriend. It's been a while since I've been in a relationship. Right now I'm unable to commit to a woman because of my erratic schedule, dividing my time at new and ongoing construction sites, business meetings in New York, and occasionally accompanying Giles to the Bahamas to oversee newly purchased islands for WDG International. We design villas for those with enough money to own a private island."

Viviana wondered how many more deals she would have to negotiate with Noah before he left The Falls for good. She had to submit an application to reverse her property from commercial to residential so he would get approval to build on the eight acres. And after suggesting she close down the B and B, he'd offered a short-term loan for her to pay her employees during the transitional period. He had also proposed another deal: become his plus-one for a wedding scheduled a month away. The last deal was the easiest to consider because she had time to agree to or decline his offer. Right now she didn't trust him and saw Noah as manipulative.

"You don't have to give me an answer now." Noah's voice broke into her musings.

"I have no intention of giving you an answer now, because I don't know you and more importantly I don't trust you," Viviana stated firmly. "I'll let you know after you return from New York. Will that give you enough time to ask someone else to be your plus-one?"

Noah glared at her. "It will give me enough time to know if I will be attending the wedding alone."

Viviana knew she had struck a nerve, but she wasn't going to apologize. It wasn't confidence but cockiness that made Noah believe he was entitled to get whatever he wanted. She didn't need to pay an investigator to do a background check on the Wainwrights. She could glean enough information about his family's business from the internet. Their company was second to Douglas Elliman Real Estate as the largest brokerage in New York, the sixth-largest real estate company nationwide, and had recently expanded beyond the States with their overseas division in the Bahamas.

"What do you want to know about me?"

She was suddenly alert. Was she that transparent that Noah was able to read her mind? "Are you an only child?"

Noah chuckled. "No. My parents have four children— three boys and a girl."

"Where do you stand in the birth order?"

"I'm number two. My brother Jordan is almost ten years older than me."

"That's quite a gap between children."

He nodded. "It took quite a few years for my parents to reconcile."

"Were they separated?"

"No. They were living together but had separate bedrooms."

Viviana didn't think she could live under the same roof as her husband and not share a bed. She had been too young to understand the dynamics between her mother and father.

"Are there ten years between you and your younger brother?"

Shaking his head, Noah laughed softly. "No. I'm four years older than Rhett, and he's four years older than Chanel."

Resting her elbow on the table, Viviana cupped her chin on the heel of her hand. "Please tell me your mother named your brother and sister after Rhett Butler from *Gone with the Wind* and the French designer Coco Chanel."

He smiled. "Why?"

"People with names of famous people or characters are a lot more memorable. When I was a girl, I used to give all of my dolls names. I gave them names of my favorite actresses or characters from my favorite books."

Noah assumed a similar pose as Viviana's when he rested his elbow on the table. "Why were you named Viviana?"

"My aunt told me my mother was obsessed with *Gone with the Wind* and decided to name me after Vivien Leigh, the actress who played Scarlett O'Hara."

"It appears as if our mothers definitely had something in common, because Christiane loved Rhett Butler."

Viviana slowly lowered her arm. "When you said your mother's name, you gave it the French pronunciation."

"That's because my maternal grandmother was French and insisted her children learn the language, so I grew up speaking English and French."

"You're fluent in French?"

"Oui, ma belle dame."

"I understood a little of what you said, but only *yes* and *lady*," Viviana admitted.

"I said 'Yes, my beautiful lady.'"

Viviana lowered her eyes. She wanted to tell Noah he was coming on a little too strong to make her feel completely comfortable with him. He'd openly admitted that he was interested in her, but she wasn't ready to offer him anything beyond friendship. The memories of her failed relationships still hadn't faded completely, and while she knew instinctually Noah was nothing like the other three men in her past, she wanted and needed to focus all of her energies on making certain the bed-and-breakfast was profitable, especially now that she would have to cease doing business until the conversions were approved.

"Did what I said make you feel uncomfortable?"

Viviana gave him a level stare. "Yes," she said truthfully. Noah's longing stares and compliments did make her feel slightly uncomfortable because the men with whom she had been involved were a lot more subtle in their approach.

However, she had to remind herself that he'd had an overabundance of confidence, beginning with who he was and his accomplishments. He was a Wainwright, born into wealth and privilege. He was able to buy and sell properties with a single keystroke. And after he'd admitted to using a portion of his own money for the sale because he liked her, Viviana felt as if he had somehow bought her.

Crossing his arms over his chest, Noah leaned back in his chair. "I'm sorry about that. What can I do to alleviate your feeling uncomfortable with me?"

"Stop trying to manipulate me into doing what you want."

Noah nodded. "Point taken."

"And if we're going to spend time together, we should feel comfortable enough with each other to say exactly what's on our mind."

He smiled. "I agree. I believe I can take whatever you dish out."

"If we hadn't eaten together this morning, I definitely would've thought that you'd had a bowl of narcissism for breakfast."

"I believe you're confusing narcissism with confidence, Viv. I know who I am and what I can and cannot do. If that makes me a narcissist, then so be it. I would never presume to tell you how to run an inn or a bed-and-breakfast because I don't have the temperament to schmooze with folks who come with a litany of complaints about what they don't like about their accommodations or the service."

"What would you tell them if they did complain?"

"I would politely tell them to check out and would wish them well finding other lodgings which suited their needs."

"That's the complete opposite of what I learned in Hospitality 101."

"In my line of work, I cannot afford to be that hospitable. I design structures in keeping with the region and what I believe people can afford. We just put up a luxury condo in a gentrified DC neighborhood geared to an upscale populace with disposable income. Many of the units were sold less than three months after we released the prospectus.

"Building here in Wickham Falls will be the first time WDG will construct homes for low- and moderately low-income families, and I'm proud to be the one to initiate it. Affordable housing is a problem that goes across race, gender and ethnicity. If WDG can be the first real estate company to tackle this crisis and hopefully shame the other big guys into doing the same, then, yes, I'm a narcissist."

"What about profits, Noah?"

"What about it, Viv?"

"Will you use inferior materials to build the homes here in The Falls to maximize profits?"

A beat passed as Noah stared at Viviana. "You still don't trust men, do you?"

She blinked slowly. "Why would you say that?"

"What do I have to do or say to get you to believe

that I'm not going to take advantage of you or any of the people who live here?"

"You don't have a problem throwing money around to get what you want, Noah. So why should I trust you?"

"Don't forget my cousin lives here. Do you think I'd do something that would negatively impact him as a Wainwright? Living in a small town is vastly different from a big city where you can go about in relative anonymity. The last thing I want is for folks to treat Giles and his family like they're pariahs."

Viviana refused to wither under his hostile stare. "I only asked because, if the structures did prove to be inferior and if they were built on land that once belonged to the Wolfes, my life would become a living hell. Did the investigator put in your report that when Lee decided to drop out of the private school and go to the public high school that no one would sit with him during lunch because he was related to the Wolfes and his father was a drug addict and a felon? That folks were quick to point the finger at my brother when he was falsely accused of breaking into someone's home because someone had stolen his jacket and left it at the scene? So, I have a right to ask you about what you intend to put up because I have to live here for the rest of my life, and I hope and pray that one day I won't be judged for who my family was."

Viviana was unaware of the tears filling her eyes and streaming down her cheeks during her fervent speech until she buried her face in her hands. She didn't know Noah pushed back his chair, rose and came around the table until his arms went around her body and held her close to his chest.

"Please don't cry, sweetheart," Noah whispered in her ear. "Everything is going to work out, and I'm not going to let anyone ever hurt you again." He buried his face in Viviana's hair, inhaling the floral scent clinging to the silky curls. He'd found her spirited and at times sharp-tongued and knew it was a defense mechanism to keep people at a distance. But then he'd discovered her Achilles' heel. Not only had she sought to protect herself but also her family. Even though she bore no responsibility for what her deceased ancestors had done to those in the region, it was apparent people had long memories and continued to blame her and her brother for others' past misdeeds.

Noah kissed her hair, but it was her mouth he wanted to taste. He wasn't a romantic and scoffed at his friends who claimed they'd fallen in love at first sight, but now he knew what they were talking about. The instant he'd walked in The Falls House and saw Viviana Remington staring back him, he knew she was the one he had been searching for. He'd purchased the land, but the zoning issue still had to be resolved. However, Noah knew that was easier to settle compared to getting Viviana to trust him enough not to take advantage of her.

The only thing he feared when introduced to Viviana was that she was involved with a man. But once he discovered she was single and unencumbered, he knew he had to work fast to make her aware of his interest in her.

Washington, DC, wasn't that far from Wickham Falls, and he'd had to call on all of his self-control not to get into his car and drive down to catch a glimpse of her with the excuse that he was coming to see Giles and his family. He'd been able to curtail his impulsiveness until the condo was completed, then had shifted his single focus to establishing a relationship with a woman who unknowingly made him rethink his lifestyle. Now he wanted what his older cousin had—a wife and a family of his own.

Viviana eased back, and Noah reached into the pocket of his jeans and took out a handkerchief and dabbed her face. His eyes caressed her face. "You're even beautiful when you cry." Her lids fluttered wildly before she closed her eyes. Fringes of long, black lashes lay on ridges of high cheekbones.

"I believe you," she whispered.

He angled his head. "What do you believe?"

She opened her eyes. "I believe that you will protect me."

Noah lowered his head and kissed her gently, and he felt that he had scaled a hurdle when she kissed him back, her lips parting slightly under his. His breathing had quickened, and he knew if he continued to kiss Viviana, it would end with him wanting to make love to her. They were the only two people in the house, and that alone made it even more tempting, but Noah did not want to take advantage of her vulnerability and be added to the string of men that had used her for their own selfish needs.

He ended the kiss. "I'm going to help you clean up

before I head back to the guesthouse. When I see you tomorrow morning, I'm going to need the payroll figures on your employees so I can—"

Viviana placed her fingers over his mouth, cutting off what he was going to say. "I don't need you to give me any money. I still have some left after the renovations and repairs. We don't know how long it's going to take for the zoning board to approve the conversions, so if I run short, then I'll let you know."

"I don't want you to run short. Take the money as a cushion. I don't need it." Noah recognized indecision in her eyes.

"Are you sure?"

He smiled. What he didn't tell Viviana was that he had enough money to take care of her and their children, grand- and great-grandchildren. "Of course I'm sure."

"Okay. I'll accept it."

Noah silently sighed with relief. He knew it would take time for Viviana to trust completely that he would not take advantage of her financially or emotionally. While he often had little patience with others, he realized he had to modify his attitude because he knew she was worth the wait.

Chapter Four

Viviana sat on a wooden bench filling out the application that would reverse the Wickham Falls Bed and Breakfast from a commercial enterprise to a residential home. The clerk at the front desk informed her that the zoning board met bimonthly and there was a backlog, so she probably wouldn't receive a letter requesting her presence until mid-January. She didn't believe the dour woman because Viviana doubted if there were *that* many applications on the board's calendar for her to wait nearly three months for a hearing. It also meant that Noah's application was also among the backlog.

He'd come over earlier that morning, and she'd given him the payroll figures on her employees; he promised to have a check deposited in her business account before the end of the day. She completed the application and watched as the clerk stamped it with a date stamp and number and printed out a receipt for her.

"Good luck, Miss Remington. May I make a suggestion?"

Viviana stared at the woman who had been a fixture at the town hall for as long as she could remember. There was something that reminded her of an animated character, with her steel-gray hair pulled back tightly in a bun and her half-glasses resting on the end of her long, straight nose. She had never seen the woman smile, and her gray eyes were cold as ashes. "Yes, Mrs. Dobbs."

"Get rid of your lodgers while you wait for the board to approve your converting your boardinghouse back to a private residence. It would look as if you're not operating in good faith if you're making money when you want to use your home for your family."

She managed what could pass for a smile. "My only guest is leaving in two days, and I've arranged to meet with my employee tomorrow morning to let them know I'm closing down until the conversion has been completed." She'd also hung a closed-for-the-season sign on the stanchion in front of the house.

A tinge of red suffused the woman's pale cheeks. "Well, it looks as if you're way ahead of me."

This time Viviana did smile. "Yes, I am. Have a wonderful day, Mrs. Dobbs."

Turning on her heel, she walked out of the building and into the warm fall sunlight and collided with a solid body. A pair of strong fingers curved around her shoulders. She glanced up and smiled. She'd bumped into Seth Collier, the sheriff of Wickham Falls. Seth, like so many young men in The Falls, had enlisted in the corps and served as military police. He'd left after twenty years and returned to The Falls. He was appointed a deputy sheriff and married Dr. Natalia Hawkins before he was eventually elected sheriff.

"I'm sorry, Sheriff Collier."

Seth pushed back the brim of the wide felt hat and smiled. "Since when did you start using titles with me? What happened to *Seth*?"

He was at least ten years older than her, and Viviana rarely interacted with him because she didn't attend Johnson County Public School.

She met a pair of light brown eyes that were almost an exact match for his complexion. "You're in uniform, so it's only right I address you by your title."

Seth smiled. "I'll give you a pass this time. By the way, how's Leland and his family doing?"

"They're well. Angela calls me at least once a week to give me an update on what's been going on with them. She says she's still attempting to adjust to her new lifestyle of getting the twins up early and out to day care before going to her classes. Leland leaves the house before her, but he does all of the cooking, and they've managed to share chores which allows them time to study."

"Attending college while taking care of a couple little ones can't be easy."

Viviana nodded. "That's why they've agreed not to add to their family until after they graduate."

"Natalia and I are working on expanding our family, so don't be surprised if there is a little Collier underfoot sometime next year."

"Good for you. I'll tell Lee you asked about him."

"When is he coming back this way?"

"I don't know. But I'm planning to go to North Carolina for Thanksgiving."

"Give him and Angela my best."

Viviana nodded. "I will. And let me know when you and your wife announce you're going to have a baby, and I'll begin piecing a quilt for the crib."

"You don't have to do that, Viviana."

"Yes, I do. Every baby should have something handmade instead of store-bought which can be passed down to the next generation. Just don't tell Natalia that I'm making it."

Seth mimed zipping his lips. "I promise not to breathe a word."

She walked around the corner to the parking at the rear of the row of stores and got into her five-year-old, off-white Honda she'd affectionately named Diamond. She rarely took it out of the garage, and despite its age there were times when she could still detect a new-car smell.

Viviana returned to the house and climbed the staircase to the attic where she had stored fabric and yarn in airtight plastic containers. Sitting on a low stool, she stared around the space. She rarely came up here anymore since her aunt and uncle had relocated to Arizona. As a child it had been her playhouse, where she talked to her dolls as if they could understand what she was saying.

It was Aunt Barbara Wolfe-McCarthy who had taught her to cook, knit, crochet and quilt. She knew her aunt wasn't her mother, but she realized her life was pretty good because Aunt Barbara worked hard to make sure she and Leland had a maternal figure.

Viviana did not want to have a pity party but knew she needed a good cry if only to rid herself of the mental and emotional baggage she had been carrying for much too long. Her eyes filled with tears, and she cried for her mother, who'd loved a man who had failed her and her children over and over, even when he knew she was dying. She cried for her father, who had fallen prey to a drug that had held him in its savage grip and had only let him go once he was behind bars. And she cried for the old Viviana who'd let her heart rule her head, even when it had been obvious her boyfriends were using her, while she always hoped it would get better.

She cried without making a sound, and when there were no more tears, she got up and went downstairs to her bedroom and washed her face in the en suite bath. She peered at her reflection in the vanity mirror and saw a face she did not quite recognize as her own. There was a steeliness in her eyes that hadn't been there before, and she knew she wasn't the same woman who'd sat in the attic crying for what was and would never be again. It was time for her to look ahead and do only what was good for Viviana Etta Remington.

An unbidden smile flitted over her features. "Damn it, girl! You had to wait until you were twenty-nine to get your act together," she said to her reflection. *Better late than never*, said the silent voice. She'd closed the B and B and had enough money to pay her employees until the end of the year. All of the bills were paid, and she had nothing but time on her hands to wait and see what was coming next. She'd told Leland she was coming to Charlotte to celebrate Thanksgiving with him, and she had confirmed with her aunt and uncle that she planned to come to Arizona to spend Christmas with them.

She thought of Noah's invitation for her to become his plus-one for a destination wedding. She still wasn't ready to tell him she would go with him because not only did she not know him well, but that they hadn't actually dated. And she didn't want to fall into the same trap as she had with the other men in her past, by becoming too trusting much too soon.

This is not to say she didn't like Noah, because she did, but it was his arrogance that he could get whatever he wanted that she found disturbing.

Yet interacting with him made her feel more in control than she had with the other men she had dated. It was as if her last relationship had taught her to say exactly what was on her mind without having to censor herself. And if she was going to go away with Noah, then it would have to be on her terms, because she had no intention of sleeping with him no matter how attractive she found him or how much money he threw at her, and she reveled in her newfound strength and resolve.

The last time she'd gone away was earlier that summer, when her friends from college had gifted her with a seven-day cruise for her birthday. Her step was light as she practically skipped down the staircase and retrieved her cell phone from her bucket bag. Viviana scrolled through the directory until she found Noah's number, tapped it and waited for a connection.

"Talk to me, sweetheart."

She smiled even though he couldn't see her. "It's *yes*."

"*Yes* to what?"

"I'll be your plus-one for the wedding."

"Hot damn! I thought I was going to go solo."

"Well, appears you're not. When are we leaving?"

"We'll fly out of New York a week from Thursday. I told you that I have to leave in a couple of days to go home for my dad's birthday, but then I'll be back. I'm going with Giles, who is driving up with Mya and Lily. They plan to stay in New York through the New Year, so I'll leave my car at your place until I come back in January. I won't need it in New York City."

"Can I drive it?"

"Of course. I'm certain it's a lot faster than your Honda."

"How dare you talk about Diamond like that?"

"You named your car?"

"Of course. Don't you name yours?"

"No, Viv. It's just a car."

If you say so, she thought. It was a car with a hundred-thousand-dollar sticker price. "I filed my application, and the clerk told me there's a backlog, and I probably won't get a hearing until mid-January," she said, deftly changing the topic.

"She said the same thing to me, and I didn't want to believe her because she kept looking at me sideways since she knew I was a stranger."

"Folks in The Falls always keep strangers at arm's length until they discover what they're up to."

"Well, I'm definitely not some snake-oil salesman looking to take their hard-earned money."

"We've had enough of those to last several lifetimes. I remember my aunt talking about her grandmother going to tent revivals, where itinerant preachers would fleece people out of their money by purportedly healing someone who wasn't really blind or disabled."

Noah's deep laugh came through the phone. "Shades of *Elmer Gantry*. Giles got a call from his Bahamian broker a couple of hours ago, saying that he should fly down to see a prospective buyer, so I'm going to stay with Mya and Lily until he comes back. I hope to see you before we leave for New York."

"It's okay, Noah. Take care of your family. We'll have plenty of time to see each other."

"Thanks for being so understanding, sweetheart."

What did he expect her to say? That he shouldn't look after his family? "We'll talk later."

Viviana ended the call without waiting for his response. What she needed to do was go through her closet to select clothes appropriate for the tropics. She'd bought a new wardrobe for her birthday cruise, but decided she needed a few outfits that were better suited for the beach. She planned to drive up to Charleston and shop until she dropped.

Edward Wainwright appeared visibly embarrassed by the display of affection as he lowered his eyes. Noah had raised his flute of champagne along with the others at the table to toast the current CEO of WDG. It had taken years for Noah to get to know his father well enough to judge his moods, which would range from affectionate to solemn and unforgiving within seconds. He'd overheard rumors that his wife had more steel in her spine than her husband and that she should've become CEO rather than Edward.

Noah loved and respected his father but felt Edward had tried too hard to please his own father, who'd literally pulled himself up by the bootstraps as a poor kid from the Lower East Side. He'd come to build a real estate empire, and he had run it like a tyrant and had only relinquished power to Edward once he felt his eldest was ready to take his place.

Edward smiled as he glanced around the table. Prisms of light from a chandelier reflected off a full head of expertly barbered silver hair. Although modest, he was extremely vain when it came to his appearance. He'd passed his blond hair and patrician features on to Noah, who could have been his father's younger clone.

"I'd like to thank everyone for coming to help me celebrate another year of life. It isn't often that I get all of my children together at the same time, but I suppose they believe this is a milestone birthday, so I thank you—Jordan, Noah, Rhett and Chanel—for thinking enough of your old man to put aside whatever you've been doing in your very busy lives to be here with me. And I include my cousins Fraser and Pat and nephews Giles, Patrick and Brandt and, of course, their incredibly beautiful wives."

Chanel rolled her eyes upward. "Now, Daddy, there's no need to get sappy."

Christiane's emerald green eyes gave off angry sparks as she glared at her daughter. "Please don't ruin the evening by being sarcastic."

Noah rested a hand on his sister's shoulder. "Let it go," he whispered in her ear.

"It's okay, Chris," Edward said to his wife, who continued to glare at Chanel. "This is a night where we're not going to get into it with one another." He stared directly at Chanel. "I've earned the right to get sappy, and when you reach my age, hopefully you'll discover that. Everyone knows I'm not one for long speeches, but starting today, I'm putting out the word that I'm giving WDG one more year, and then I'm stepping down." He shifted and looked at his nephew. "Pat, you need to prepare yourself to take over from me."

Patrick Wainwright III shook his head. "Everyone knows I want nothing to do with running the company. I like working with Dad in Legal."

"What about you, Noah?" Edward asked. "I know you're out of the office for extended periods of time overseeing your construction projects. But don't you think your engineer is capable enough to assume that responsibility?"

Noah clamped his teeth tightly to keep from telling his father he did not want to be put on the spot about a position he'd never wanted. He knew he would go stir-crazy if he had to sit behind a desk day after day. "Dad, you're asking people you know don't want to run the company. I like what I'm doing, and so does Pat. What you're not doing is looking at the ones who may have a new vision to take WDG in another direction. Look at what Giles has done with the international division."

"What other direction is there?" Wyatt Wainwright asked.

Everyone turned to look at Wyatt, the family's patriarch. Noah had always likened his grandfather to a hawk. The black hair was now snow-white, and his piercing blue eyes were still as clear and sharp as a raptor's. He had prided himself on his ability to stare down and intimidate business rivals and subsequently get them to do his bidding.

"There's never one direction, Grandpa, when it comes to business," Noah said. "People no longer have to get into their cars to buy anything they want, because of online retail. There are apps for real estate companies where folks go online and decide what properties they want to look at even before contacting a broker. WDG has been a giant in real estate, but there are things we still need to change."

Wyatt angled his head. "What are you trying to say?"

Noah successfully hid a smile when he took a sip of champagne. In the past his grandfather would've exploded if someone had challenged him, but now that he was in his eighties, he'd mellowed somewhat. "We've done well buying foreclosed properties and renovating them into luxury units with selling prices beginning at six figures. For every luxury building we put up, we also need to build affordable housing."

"Like you plan to do in Wicky Falls?" Edward asked.

"It's *Wickham Falls*," Noah and Giles said in unison.

"Sorry about that," Edward apologized. "Please continue, Noah."

"I've discussed this with Rhett and Chanel, and they agree with me because now it's not all about profits but making people realize their American dream with home ownership. Dad, you should bring Rhett and Chanel on, and train them to take over as CEO and COO. Rhett is well-versed in real estate law, and don't forget Chanel graduated at the top of her class with a degree in business and finance. It's about time a Wainwright woman is granted a seat on the board of directors." He did smile when he saw Mya and Jordan's wife, Aziza, nudge each other.

"I like that idea," Christiane said, smiling. She'd recently had her stylist cut her platinum hair into a becoming bob that flattered her oval face.

"Of course you would," Edward countered, "because they are your kids."

"And yours, too, Teddy," she retorted. She looked across the table at her father-in-law. "Grandpa, what do you think of Noah's suggestion?"

"It just might work."

"Of course it will work, Grandpa," Noah said. "It's time to infuse some young Wainwright blood into the company." Although WDG employed hundreds, only Wainwrights were permitted to sit on the board of directors.

"Noah's right," Fraser Wainwright interjected. "My

kids have no interest in real estate, so that leaves Teddy's and Patrick's children."

Edward gave each person sitting around the table in the formal dining room a long, penetrating look. "Don't you think it's time for Chanel and Rhett to speak for themselves?"

Rhett, four years younger than Noah, smiled at his sister. "I know I've told everyone before that I prefer practicing law with Jordan, but I'm willing to step up if Dad needs me."

"The same with me," Chanel said in agreement. "Even though I just started working at the investment bank, and I don't think they're going to be too happy about me leaving."

"It's not as if you need them for a reference," Giles said, deadpan. He smiled and bumped fists with Jordan.

A beat passed, and then Chanel said, "Noah's right about having a woman on the board, but I'll only accept it if Aziza joins me. And because she's married to Jordan, and that makes her a Wainwright."

Aziza Fleming-Wainwright looked like a deer caught in the glare of headlights when she stared at Chanel. The tall, beautiful African American attorney was the mother of a one-year-old. "I can't."

"Why not?" Chanel asked. "I know you have Maxwell, but I'm certain my mother would be willing to look—"

"Of course I would love to babysit him," Christiane said, cutting off Chanel. She doted on her only grandchild.

Aziza whispered something to Jordan and then nodded. "I'm willing to come on board, but only for two and no more than three days a week until Maxwell goes to nursery school."

Noah leaned back in his chair, crossed his arms over his chest and affected a smug grin as he congratulated himself for shattering decades of a male-only boards of directors by suggesting his sister join the company.

Edward stood up, with everyone following suit when he lifted his flute. "This calls for another toast." He nodded to Aziza, Rhett and Chanel. "This is definitely a new day for the Wainwright Developers Group. Welcome aboard."

Noah excused himself before dessert was served and walked out of the dining room. He took a back staircase to his second-floor suite. There hadn't been a reason for him to move out of the house where he'd grown up, because all of his needs were met by an efficient household staff.

He'd done all of the driving from West Virginia to New York City because Giles had returned to Wickham Falls from the Bahamas on a red-eye earlier that morning and had spent the trip sleeping on the minivan's third-row seat. Giles had spent four days in the Bahamas and had asked Noah to go back with him to meet with the owner of a new island who wanted him to design villas reminiscent of those in Bali. He'd agreed, even though he wanted to spend time with Viviana before they jetted off to the wedding.

He'd got to see Viviana briefly earlier that morning

when he dropped off his car and retrieved his laptop and printer from the guesthouse, before she drove him back to Giles and Mya's house. He'd resisted the urge to kiss her when he saw Mya standing on the porch holding her daughter, not wanting to embarrass her with a public display of affection.

Noah walked into the en suite bath, showered and changed into a pair of sweatpants with a matching Yale T-shirt. He had settled himself on the sofa when he heard a knock on the door. "Come in."

Christiane had also exchanged her dress and heels for a pair of slacks and a loose-fitting blouse. "Would you like some company?"

Noah patted the cushion beside him. "Come and sit down, Mom." The familiar scent of Chanel No. 5 wafted to his nostrils when she sat. It was the only fragrance he had ever known her to wear. He dropped an arm over her shoulders. Christiane Johnston had come from old money, while the Wainwrights were new money—a fact that Wyatt, the Wainwright patriarch, was never allowed to forget whenever he interacted with his daughter-in-law's family.

Christiane patted his knee. "I like what you did at dinner. I've been trying to get your father to include Chanel in the business, but the old bull just wouldn't budge. He's too much like his father and believes women are only good enough to bear their children and host dinner parties."

"That may be Grandpa's way of thinking, but it's not the same with Dad. It's just that there are so many

Wainwright men that the women are overwhelmed when all they hear is talk about buying and selling properties."

"Did Chanel tell you she wanted to join the company?"

Noah shook his head. "Not in so many words. I think she was a little upset when she had to apply for positions outside of WDG when Dad could've created one for her. It's the same with Rhett. There was no reason he had to join Jordan's law practice when he could work with Patrick."

"You have to know that Rhett doesn't get along very well with his uncle."

"Well, they'll have to learn to get along once Rhett becomes CEO."

Christiane sighed. "I hope you're right. Now, tell me about what's going on in West Virginia."

"Nothing much at this time because I've hit a snag obtaining permits with the town's zoning board."

"I'm not talking about your construction project."

Noah met his mother's eyes. "What are you talking about?"

"When I asked you last week how long you were going to be here, you said only a few days because you're flying down to the Bahamas with Giles, then you were going back to West Virginia. When are you going to stay home for more than a few days?"

"I'll be here for two days, and then I'm going back to the Bahamas with Giles because one of his clients wants me to design several villas for his new resort."

"Once you come back, can you spare some time for your old mother?"

Noah kissed her cheek. "There's nothing about you that's old." Christiane was sixty-three but looked years younger, and he suspected his mother was seeing her dermatologist for injections of fillers. "I can't promise you that I'll have enough time to hang out here because I'm invited to a destination wedding in the Bahamas over the Veterans Day holiday weekend."

"And what do you intend to do after that?"

"I don't know, Mom." He knew he wouldn't be granted a hearing with the zoning board until mid-January, so he did not project what he would be doing that far in advance.

Christiane touched the area around her eyes with her fingertips. "Will I at least see you for Thanksgiving and Christmas? Even Giles and Mya plan to stay in New York until January, and I thought you would also stay."

"The only thing I'm going to promise is I'll be back for Thanksgiving and Christmas."

A beat passed. "Is there someone who has caught your eye?"

Noah recalled telling Viviana that he did not lie to his parents. "Yes."

"Is she nice?"

He smiled. His mother always asked if he'd met a nice girl. "Yes, Mom. She's very nice."

"Nice enough to marry?"

"You're getting ahead of yourself. I just met her, and we have yet to have what I'd call an official date."

Christiane crossed her feet at the ankles. "I just hope you don't date her for a while and then drop her like you've done with the others."

"I stopped seeing the others because I didn't like them enough to commit."

"And are you willing to commit to this young woman?"

Noah frowned. "Stop it with the interrogation, Mom. I know what you're up to. You want more grandchildren. Isn't Maxwell enough?"

"No. I want more because most of those in my social circle have at least three or four to my one."

"Please don't tell me that you and your friends compete as to who has the most grandchildren."

"Giles's mother, Amanda, couldn't wait to call me to say she now has grandsons *and* a granddaughter. And once Giles told her Mya was pregnant, she invited me to lunch and cackled like a hen laying an egg that she was going to get another grandbaby. If we weren't family, I would've given her a good cursing out for gloating like she did."

Noah kissed his mother's hair. "You shouldn't let her upset you. I'm certain Jordan and Aziza will have more kids, and one of these days Rhett and Chanel will also marry and give you all the grandbabies you'd ever want or need."

"What about you, Noah? Don't you want to marry and have children?"

"Yes."

Christiane smiled. "Are you telling me my wild child is finally ready to settle down?"

Noah had always resented his mother when she referred to him as her *wild child*. He thought of himself as a restless spirit. It was as if he couldn't stay in one place for more than a few weeks at a time. And whenever he felt as if he were being smothered, he'd fly down to the family's Bahamian island resort and stay there, living his life.

"You'll just have to wait and see, won't you, Mom?" he said cryptically.

"Yes, I will," Christiane said as she rested her head on her son's shoulder. She sighed. "I know you're tired, so I'm going to leave so you can get some rest. Will you join us for breakfast?"

Noah dropped another kiss on his mother's hair. "Of course." He assisted her in standing and walked her to the door, closing and locking it behind her. It wasn't quite nine o'clock, but he was ready to turn in for the night. He shut off his cell, dimmed the table lamp in the living/dining area, walked into the bedroom, stripped off his clothes and got into bed. The sounds of vehicular traffic along Fifth Avenue sounded abnormally loud when he compared it to the silence he'd encountered in Wickham Falls.

He punched the pillow under his head, and after tossing and turning restlessly for ten minutes, Noah stared up at the ceiling. Reaching over, he picked the remote off the bedside table. He clicked on the wall-mounted television, scrolling through the program guide for a movie he hadn't seen before.

Noah finally selected one starring Dwayne Johnson and settled down to watch his favorite action-hero actor do what he did best: rescue those in danger. He set the sleep timer, and after twenty minutes his eyes closed and he never saw when the movie ended and the credits rolled across the screen before going dark.

Chapter Five

Viviana waited on the porch with her luggage for the car service. Noah had called to tell her he was sending a driver to pick her up and take her to the Tri-State Airport, where he would meet her for their trip to the Bahamas.

She'd armed the security system and reprogrammed the timers on the lights, and the day before she had contacted Seth to let him know she would be out of town and to keep an eye on her property. He'd laughed, telling her he was also watching Giles and Mya's house, which was across the street from his, until they returned from New York. He then promised to have one of his deputies stop by to check on her house at least once or twice a day. The opioid epidemic hadn't passed Wickham Falls by, and home break-ins were more frequent. When she had contracted with the security company, Viviana had the technician install cameras around the exterior of the property, with no-delay motion detectors on the side and rear doors, and program the system directly to the sheriff, fire and local doctors' offices.

She had also called her brother, giving Leland an update about the issues facing Noah's inability to build on the property they'd sold him. He encouraged her to stay positive, and if she needed him for anything, then all she had to do was call. She did tell him she was going away for a week but did not disclose who she was going with or where. Leland told her to be sure to have fun and that he would see her for Thanksgiving.

The driver pulled up, popped the trunk to the town car, got out and opened a rear door. "Good morning, Miss Remington."

Viviana smiled. "Good morning."

She settled herself on the leather seat, while the driver loaded her bags into the trunk. Viviana knew she had packed too many clothes for a long weekend, but she couldn't resist not bringing some of the outfits she'd purchased during her shopping spree at her favorite Charleston boutique. She had selected several dresses, shorts, slacks, blouses and caftans, as well as bikini and one-piece swimsuits. The wedding was scheduled for Saturday, and Noah said some of the guests were flying in on Thursday to avoid the airport holiday crush. She and Noah would spend six days together before she returned to The Falls.

The drive to the regional airport was a lot quicker

than the hour-long one to Charleston. Viviana peered out of the side window when the driver maneuvered into the airport, where he handed security personnel a document. The man peered into the window, stared at her and then asked for her passport. After scanning the bar code on the inside of the back page, he stamped a page, returned her passport, punched in a code that opened the gate and waved for the driver to pass through. Within minutes, she spied Noah on the tarmac talking to a pilot outside a gleaming white private jet. When she'd asked him about a ticket, he'd told her he would take care of all of her travel documents and that she only had to bring her passport. She smiled when he walked over to open the rear door.

His face was deeply tanned and his hair nearly bleached white from his time in the hot sun. "Now I know why I don't have a ticket." She'd noticed *WDG* and several numbers painted on the aircraft's tail.

Noah extended his hand and helped Viviana out of the car. She wore a pair of pale blue cropped pants, a matching off-the-shoulder ruffled blouse that left her flat belly exposed and a pair of blue-and-white-striped espadrilles with laces encircling her slim ankles. He lowered his head and brushed a light kiss over her mouth, then leaned back to study her face as if committing it to memory. He hadn't realized how much he'd missed her until now. When Viviana had called to tell him she would be his plus-one he did not want to believe she had changed her mind, and whispered a prayer of thanks that she had. He'd attempted to recall everything about her, but failed miserably. She was more beautiful than he had remembered.

After spending two days with his mother, he and Giles had boarded a jet for a flight to the Wainwright resort to meet with a wealthy client who'd recently purchased a ten-acre island from WDG International as an investment on which he wanted Noah to design private villas. It had been more than a week before the eccentric billionaire had finally approved the design of villas built over the water.

"I've missed you so much," he whispered for her ears only.

"Me, too," Viviana said, as her arms went around his waist.

Noah stared over her head. It had taken spending time away from Viviana and Wickham Falls to figure out what he wanted and needed for his future. It was no longer about doing what made him happy but how he could make someone else equally happy.

"Come on, sweetheart. The tower has cleared the pilot for takeoff." He slipped the driver a generous tip after he'd handed off Viviana's bag to the pilot. Holding her hand, he escorted her up the steps of the jet and into the cabin.

A flight attendant greeted Viviana with a friendly smile. "Welcome aboard, Ms. Remington. As soon as you are seated and belted in, we will be on our way. Once we reach cruising altitude, the crew will serve breakfast. You'll find the menu on your seat."

Noah showed Viviana to a seat in the aircraft and waited until she was seated and belted in before turning his chair to face her. He had to admit she looked well. Her face was fuller than it had been when he'd last seen her. She had brushed her curly hair off her face and styled it in a single braid. Her large brown eyes stared at him.

"What are you thinking about?"

She blinked slowly. "This jet belongs to your company."

Noah nodded. "We always use it for business travel."

Her mouth softened when she smiled. "Is this a business trip?"

Lines fanned out around Noah's eyes when he smiled. "It will be if you agree to go with me to one of WDG's vacation resorts."

"How many resorts do you have?"

"Only two."

"You say *only two* like answering someone who's asked what time it is."

"It didn't start out that way. When I was a kid, my family alternated years flying down to the Caribbean for the week between Christmas and New Year's with holding a week-long celebration in New York. One day, my grandfather decided it was time to build a house in the Bahamas large enough to accommodate the entire Wainwright clan. But then he changed his mind when he read an article in a travel magazine about hundreds of private islands that were up for sale. He negotiated with the Bahamian government and bought one close to twenty acres and constructed an airstrip for those wishing to fly in. He built the house and then a number of villas for vacationers. Once Giles resigned his commission in the military and joined WDG, he established the international division and has been busy buying and selling islands to those with enough money and who want their own private playgrounds."

Viviana's hands tightened on the armrests when the jet picked up speed before lifting off. "How often do you go there?"

"I just got back. WDG's broker lives on the premises, and it's where we always conduct business. After we leave the island where the wedding is taking place, we can catch a boat and go to Emerald Cove."

"Why is it called Emerald Cove?" Viviana questioned.

"Technically, the Bahamas are in the Atlantic Ocean but are near the Caribbean Sea where some of the waters are more green than gray. The water near my family's resort tends to appear green, hence the name. If you don't have anything planned back in Wickham Falls, we can extend our stay for at least another week." He held up a hand. "You don't have to give me your answer now. We'll take it day by day and see how well we get along."

Her eyebrows lifted. "You doubt we'll get along?"

"I've made it a practice never to make presumptions, because it just might backfire."

"If that's the case, then I'll wait until after the wedding to give you my answer."

It was the second time she would make Noah wait for her answer. In the past, she would've jumped at the suggestion or invitation, but that was the old Viviana. She had been so willing to please other people, even to her own detriment. When she'd asked her aunt why boys and men tended to take advantage of her, Viviana was shocked when Aunt Babs said she was no different than her deceased mother. Annette had fallen in love with Emory, and despite his inability to take care of his family once he'd spiraled downward, she'd never stopped loving him. Viviana was aware that her mother's sister hated what Emory had done to his wife and children, but she'd never heard Babs say a bad word against him out of respect for Annette and her niece and nephew.

Viviana gazed out the small oval window to avoid staring at Noah. Everything about him was so very different from the men in her past that there were times when she believed she had conjured him up. That he was the prince in the fairy tales she had read as a child, when she pretended she was a princess and they would live happily ever after. And once she'd entered adolescence, she'd graduated to romance novels.

They had become her guilty pleasure, and there had never been a time when there wasn't a paperback in her bag. Her reading taste did not change in college.

Her musings were interrupted when the blue-suited male flight attendant came to take her breakfast order, and after a sumptuous breakfast of a spinach and feta omelet, prosciutto-wrapped melon and flutes of mimosas, she reclined her seat into a bed and fell asleep.

Viviana was totally disoriented when she felt someone shake her awake. She opened her eyes to find Noah leaning over her. He had covered her body with a cashmere throw. "Are we there yet?"

He smiled, his teeth very white in his sun-browned face. "Soon. You have to sit up because they're preparing to descend." He helped her pull up her seat, and she fastened her seat belt. With wide eyes, she stared out the window at the ocean surrounding lush green islands. As the jet began its descent, she saw a stretch of beach, red-tiled roofs of buildings and a section of the island where a number of boats were moored.

Her gaze swung back to Noah's as she stretched her arms over her head. The midriff top displayed more skin on her rib cage. "How long was I asleep?"

Noah found himself staring at the expanse of silken skin on Viviana's midsection. Did she have any idea of how tempting she was? He hadn't slept with a woman in months before meeting Viviana for the first time in August, and although he had gone through long periods when he had been celibate, he hadn't found himself as tested as he was now.

"Well over an hour."

She smiled, bringing his gaze to linger on her full parted lips. "I hope I didn't snore."

He winked at her. "You didn't." Viviana ran a hand over her hair and tucked several strands behind her ears that had escaped the plait. Noah liked her hair when she didn't wear a braid or ponytail. Unbound, it reminded him of photos of Cher with a cascade of black curls floating around her face and shoulders. The investigators had uncovered photographs of her mother and father, and it was apparent Viviana had inherited their best physical characteristics.

Noah was filled with an awakening sense of pride

that he could claim Viviana as his for six days, and perhaps even longer if she agreed to an extended stay at Emerald Cove. And he knew bringing her with him as his date was certain to generate a lot of talk among his friends. The last time he brought a date to a wedding had been more than two years ago.

The plane landed smoothly, and the pilot taxied along the runway until coming to a complete stop several hundred feet from a large building, where they would be processed to enter the island. Passengers from another aircraft were also deplaning and making their way toward the building where they would have to go through customs. When the light with the symbol to fasten their seat belts was extinguished, Noah unbuckled his belt and waited for Viviana to do the same.

He reached for her hand as she gathered her wristlet. He thanked the flight crew and assisted Viviana as they walked down the stairs, stepping onto the tarmac which held the heat from the blazing tropical sun. The flight crew had set their bags on the tarmac for them.

Noah waved to a young man holding up a sign, who had a dolly loaded with other bags. He wore a name tag identifying him as Charles. "We're going to the Governor's House." He pointed to the bags near the jet. "Those are ours."

Charles nodded. "I will wait until you are cleared through customs, then I will load your bags on the van going to the Governor's House."

Noah inclined his head. "Thank you." His friend's fiancée's family had chosen the resort because it was smaller than the others on the island and everything was inclusive. He gave Viviana's fingers a gentle squeeze. "I hope you packed sunblock."

She nodded. "But of course. How far is the resort from the airport?"

Noah led her toward the building and removed his passport from the back pocket of his sand-colored linen slacks. "It's about a fifteen-minute drive from here."

She glanced up at him. "You've been here before?"

"Once, when I decided to do some island-hopping."

"You must have been quite the party animal back in the day."

Noah stared straight ahead as the line moved slowly. "I must admit I've done my share of partying."

"How hard?"

He gave Viviana a sidelong glance, wondering how much he wanted to tell her about his past when he'd come to know hers based on the investigator's report. "Very hard."

Her eyebrows lifted slightly. "Have you gotten it out of your system?"

He smiled. "Oh yeah. It was either stop or burn out completely."

"What made you stop?" she asked.

"It was a combination of things," Noah said. "My father had started talking about retiring, and I knew it was time for me to step up to the table and do my part. My parents weren't very happy about my lifestyle, and constantly reminded me of it."

"Where were you living at the time?"

"I have a suite in the house where I grew up."

Viviana gave him an incredulous stare. "You still live at home?"

"Yes. I decided why move out when all my needs are met."

"In other words, you have *help*."

Noah registered the condescension in her voice and wondered if she harbored some disdain for wealthy people because of how her ancestors had treated those who'd worked in their mines. "Yes. I've grown up with household *employees*," he said, stressing the word. "Many of whom have been with us for many years before they retire with a generous pension." He paused. "Can you answer one question for me?"

"What's that?"

"Does it bother you that I come from a wealthy family?"

She'd answered his question with one of her own. "Does it bother you?"

"No, it doesn't," Noah said, as they moved closer to the officials checking and stamping passports. "I must admit it has a lot of advantages, along with some drawbacks."

"What do you consider a drawback?" Viviana asked.

"That people believe you're unscrupulous and would do anything to hold on to your wealth."

"Are you referring to the Wickham Falls Wolfes?"

"You said it, Viviana, not me. It's true my grandfather did things to build his real estate empire I probably never would've imagined doing. That's something he has to deal with when searching his conscience. One thing I refuse to do is apologize for being a Wainwright. Every New Year's Eve, we host a fund-raiser and earmark the monies raised to a particular charity."

She met his eyes. "So, you do give back."

He smiled. "Big-time. What is money for if not to spend? None of us can take it with us."

Viviana nodded. "I've heard people say they've never seen an armored car following a hearse to the cemetery."

Noah laughed. "Well, it's obvious the pharaohs did not know this when they were buried with all of their worldly goods." He squeezed her hand again. "You need to rid yourself of the guilt of the Wolfes who were SOBs."

"That's easy for you say, but folks in The Falls have long memories when it comes to us. It was one of the reasons why we didn't go to the local schools. I don't know how Leland was able to take the isolation when he transferred to the high school, but somehow he endured it."

"If your brother became an Army Ranger, then he had to have the mental fortitude to survive that intense training. Don't sell yourself short, sweetheart. You're much tougher than you think. If not, then you would've left Wickham Falls."

"I don't know why, but I've never thought of leaving."

"If you were to move, then you'd have start over from scratch with a new home and employment. There's no doubt you could get a position with a hotel chain, but is that what you want when you have the advantage of being your own boss and growing your business?"

"I know once I reopen the B and B it's going to be a success because I've changed a lot since running the boardinghouse."

Noah wanted to tell her that he liked her just the way she was and there was no need for her to change. It was why he found himself falling in love with her.

They made it to the head of the line, and he handed his passport to one official, while the other asked for Viviana's. He paid the nominal entrance fee, and they got their passports stamped and walked over to where Charles waited with their luggage.

They followed him to a van filled with other passengers waiting to go to the resort and got in. Charles slipped behind the wheel, started the engine and then drove away from the airport as Viviana slipped her hand into Noah's. They shared a smile before he looked away.

Chapter Six

Viviana heard the tapping on the door connecting her suite to Noah's. She was awed by the layout of the resort, with three hundred sixty degrees of unobstructed views of the beach and ocean. Each villa was environmentally friendly and constructed with natural materials found on the island, from the bamboo walls to the thatched roofs.

She walked barefoot across the highly polished mahogany floor to open the door. Noah had changed into a pair of white linen shorts and matching short-sleeved shirt. He'd slipped his feet into a pair of tan woven sandals. His arms, legs and feet were so tanned that the color nearly matched hers.

"Please come in. I just have to comb my hair, and then I'm all yours." Once they'd arrived, Viviana hadn't bothered to unpack. Showering and shampooing her hair had taken precedence. After slathering on a layer of sunblock, she slipped on a pale pink crinkle-cotton sundress and bone-colored ballet flats. "What's the matter?" she asked when she noticed Noah staring at her with a strange look on his face.

"Do you plan to put your hair up?"

"I will, but only after it dries. Why?"

He moved closer until they were only inches apart. "Because I like your hair when you wear it down."

Viviana ran her fingers through the damp strands that fell over her shoulders like curly ribbons. "You like long hair."

"Not as much as I like you."

She felt her pulse quicken, and Viviana knew Noah had confessed what she did not want to acknowledge. She found herself talking about anything inane to keep from telling Noah how she had come to emotionally depend on him. And she did not need a therapist to tell her the men she had chosen to share her life with were a substitute for her father, who hadn't been there for her. Not only were they much older but they immediately recognized her neediness. They were willing to put up with her clinginess because it boosted their egos when seen with a much younger woman.

She wanted to feel differently about Noah, but there was something about him that wouldn't allow her to lower her defenses to trust him completely.

Viviana closed her eyes when she saw his darken to a deep moss-green. "You like me, and I like you." She opened her eyes. "Where do we go from here?"

Cradling her face in his hands, Noah pressed a kiss to her forehead. "We'll take it slow, sweetheart. I'm not going anywhere, and neither are you. That means we have all the time in the world to figure this out. I know you've been hurt, and you're probably still hurting, so it's going to be up to you to let me know when you're ready to let me into your life."

Viviana rested her head on his shoulder. "You're already in."

Anchoring his hand under her chin, he forced her to look at him. "Okay."

"Okay?"

"Yes. Okay. I'm more than willing to let you drive this relationship to wherever you want it to go. And because we'll be spending a lot of time together here and back in Wickham Falls, as the expression goes, the ball is in your court." He winked at her. "I'll be outside on the veranda."

Viviana smiled. Now she knew the ground rules for their relationship. It would be the first time she would be able to control the direction in which she wanted a liaison with a man to go. She was in the process of getting her life back on track, and she did want anything to derail it.

Returning to the bathroom, she sprayed her hair with a detangler and massaged it in, and then picked up a wide-tooth comb and ran it smoothly through the damp strands. Viviana washed her hands and dried them on a towel stamped with the resort's logo. Everything in the suite focused on a guest's convenience and satisfaction. They'd provided a collection of beauty

products available to clients in upscale spas. A brochure in the room outlined the amenities, ranging from
beauty and feminine products, bathrobes, swimwear
and a salon for haircuts, facials and manicures. There
was even a boutique for casual and evening wear.

She slid back the door leading out to the veranda
and found Noah sitting under an umbrella at a round
table and talking with several men. They were all holding drinks. Closer to the beach, a group of women had
gathered under a nearby thatched gazebo and sipped
from colorful, frothy beverages. Noah's back was to
her, but he glanced over his shoulder and stood up
when he saw the gazes of the other men move toward
her. She gave him an inviting smile with his approach.
Viviana curved an arm around his waist as his eyes
lingered on the unbound hair flowing down her back.

"Is the hair okay?" she whispered. The look in his
eyes confirmed his approval.

"Yes. Come. Let me introduce you to the ones who
came down early."

Viviana noted four pairs of eyes watching her as
Noah draped a proprietary arm over her shoulders. She
knew in a single glance that they were more than curious as to who she was. The women who'd also seen
her left the gazebo to join their male counterparts. She
noticed all of them wore wedding rings and wondered
if Noah was the only one among the group who was
still single. As she waited for Noah to make the intro-
ductions, Viviana saw the women had linked arms or
held hands with their husbands.

Noah pulled her closer to his side. "Ladies and gentlemen, it gives me the greatest pleasure to introduce you to Viviana Remington. I'm not going to tell her your names because she'll have several days to get to know who you are."

"Why don't you let the lady speak for herself?" said a tall, slender man whose fair skin was turning a bright red from the hot sun.

A gorgeous black man with a shaved head extended his hand. "I'm Brandon Benson, but everyone calls me BB."

His equally beautiful wife gave him a warning look before she flashed a facetious smile. "You'll have to excuse my husband." She offered Viviana her hand. "I'm Alicia."

Viviana shook the proffered hand. "It's nice meeting you, Alicia." One by one, the men and women introduced themselves as she attempted to commit to memory the name for each face, then gave up all together. Noah was right. She had time to learn their names before the weekend was over.

A petite curvy blonde took her hand. "Come and sit with us. Let her go, Noah," she said when he continued to hold on to Viviana's hand. "Don't worry. We're not going to kidnap her."

Viviana blew Noah an air kiss. "Don't worry, darling. I'm not going to run away." She knew she had shocked him when his mouth opened but didn't say anything. The endearment was as much for him as the others in his group. She had announced they were a couple.

She slid onto a bench in the gazebo, her eyes measuring the four women staring back at her. "I suppose you're a little curious about me," Viviana said, taking the initiative.

Alicia tossed a profusion of braided extensions over her shoulder. "I'm more than curious, but before we begin our inquisition, I think it's only polite if we introduce ourselves more fully. I'm Alicia, and Brandon and I own several fast-food franchises in St. Louis, Missouri."

"And I'm Michelle," the blonde said in introduction. "I'm married to Trace Brown. We live in Dallas. He's a DA, and I'm currently a homemaker with three little ones." She closed her eyes and waved a hand. "I love my mama-in-law for looking after them so Trace and I could have a little R & R for a few days."

Viviana smiled. "There are truly angels here on earth."

"Amen," Michelle drawled.

An attractive brunette with red-gold highlights turned on a hundred-watt smile. She'd pushed her sunglasses up on her head to reveal sparkling hazel eyes. "I'm Lynette. And the dude over there with the bulging muscles and tank top is my husband. Phil and I own a sports-therapy clinic in Miami. Now, tell us how you hooked up with Noah."

"Hold up, Lynn. Let me introduce myself before you get into the woman's business," said a tall, thin black woman with cropped silver hair. Viviana laughed along with Alicia and Michelle.

"Sorry about that," Lynette said.

"I'm Sandra Daniels, Richard's better half. And

I'm proud to say I've been cancer-free for more than a year."

Viviana leaned over and hugged Sandra. "Good for you."

Sandra had survived when Viviana's mother hadn't. After complaining of headaches and a number of unexplainable falls, Annette Remington had been diagnosed with an inoperable brain cancer which had led to her death before her thirtieth birthday.

Sandra ran a hand over her shorn head. "Thank you. Once I began chemo and started to lose my hair, I decided to cut it off, and because I'm graying prematurely, I dye it."

"You have the head and face for short hair," Viviana said.

Alicia draped an arm around Sandra's shoulders. "That's because my beautiful sister girl used to be a model. I've been after her to start modeling again, but she claims she's done."

Sandra glared at Alicia. "You're worse than a dog with a bone. We're not here to talk about me modeling again but to get to know Viviana."

"Before we begin interrogating Noah's girlfriend, would you like something to drink?" Lynette asked. She pointed to three carafes. "We have margaritas, rum punch and mai tais. Pick your poison."

Viviana turned over a glass on the tablecloth and handed it to Lynette. "I'll have a little of the rum punch. I usually don't drink on an empty stomach."

Sandra laughed. "Not to worry, girlfriend. We've

already ordered everything on the appetizer menu. It should be here at any moment."

The words were barely off her lips when two waiters carrying trays on their shoulders appeared. One stopped at the table with Noah and his friends and the other at Viviana's. Although she had eaten breakfast, the aromas wafting from the appetizers retriggered her appetite.

She filled her plate with pot stickers, sesame sushi rolls, crispy fried calamari, mint-marinated lamb kebabs with tahini and honey dip, and ginger-orange pork skewers. Sandra had been truthful about ordering everything on the menu. There were small plates of curried-coconut chicken sticks, prosciutto-wrapped figs, cheese balls, miniature empanadas with a chunky avocado relish, and filo tartlets with shrimp.

Viviana raised her glass of punch along with the other four women as they toasted old and new friendship. She took a sip of the delicious icy cocktail, wondering if they were welcoming her as a friend only because of her association with Noah and how many of his other girlfriends they had also welcomed.

The rum punch, although potent, was delicious and the appetizers yummy. Everything she ate had been perfectly prepared. She touched the corners of her mouth with a napkin. "What do you want to know about me?" Viviana knew she had caught the other women off guard when she decided to reintroduce the subject.

Sandra angled her head as she stared at Viviana under lowered lids. "How long have you known Noah?"

"Four months."

"How did you meet?" Lynette asked.

"His cousin introduced us."

She had no intention of revealing it was a business deal that had brought the two of them together. And she hadn't lied about Giles introducing her and Leland to Noah when they'd mentioned to Giles about selling off a parcel of undeveloped land they had no intention of using.

Michelle narrowed her eyes. "Do I detect a trace of the South in your voice?"

"Guilty as charged. I'm from West Virginia." Viviana wanted to remind Michelle that although her state was below the Mason-Dixon Line, West Virginians had fought alongside the Union Army during the Civil War.

Alicia sat straight. "Where in West Virginia are you from?"

"Wickham Falls. It's in the southern part of the state. It's not far from Beckley."

"I know Beckley well because I grew up in White Sulphur Springs." Alicia reached over and fist-bumped Viviana. "I knew we were sisters. I go back home at least twice a year to visit family."

Lynette popped a tiny shrimp into her mouth. "What do you do when you're not hanging out with your gorgeous boyfriend?"

"I own and operate a bed-and-breakfast in my hometown. Right now I'm closed for the season and plan to reopen in the spring."

Lynette pressed her palms together. "My grandparents owned a B and B in Tennessee, and I'd always wanted to run it, but that dream died when I fell in love with Phil and moved to Florida."

"What happened to the B and B?" Viviana asked.

"They sold it to some folks who tore it down to build a mega church."

Viviana shook her head. "I have no intention of ever selling my home." She'd gotten her brother to agree that the house and the property were to remain in their family for perpetuity.

Lynette rested her elbows on the table. "The four of us usually get together for a girls' weekend at least once a year. Maybe we'll call you and make arrangements to come to your B and B, and you can show us a little Mountain State hospitality."

"I'd truly love that. I'll give y'all my number before we leave."

Michelle pointed at Viviana. "Now I know you're a true Southern sister since you said *y'all*."

There was something about the four women Viviana liked. It was apparent they were close friends and seemingly had welcomed her into their cloistered circle. "How do you know Noah?" It was her turn to ask questions.

Sandra decided to answer for the quartet when she said, "Our husbands met Noah when they were at Yale. They weren't in what you would call an official fraternity, but they had formed their own circle where they refused to let anyone else in. We've all been to his family's resort on Emerald Cove, and if you haven't been, then you have to ask him to take you there."

He has invited me, Viviana thought. "I'm looking forward to it," she said instead.

"Are you and Noah serious?" Michelle questioned.

"Why would you ask me that?"

Michelle glanced at the others around the table. "Because it has been at least two years since we've seen Noah with a woman. Before that, he was quite the playboy. Every time we got together, he'd introduce us to a different woman. After a while, it was impossible to remember all their names."

Lynette frowned. "Viviana doesn't need to hear you talk about her boyfriend's past."

"How do you know that she hasn't already heard it?" Michelle retorted, her voice rising slightly.

"Lynn's right," Sandra said. "I'm certain Phil hasn't given you a play-by-play about all of the women he's slept with."

Viviana held up her hands. "Ladies, please stop. Noah and I don't have any secrets between us," she lied smoothly. "I know that if I hadn't agreed to be his date for this wedding, he would've come alone."

"Which makes you very, very special," Sandra stated firmly. "I'm not ashamed to say that if Noah had given me a second look, I would've scooped him up like a spoonful of my grandmama's famous mac and cheese."

Michelle smiled. "And her grandmother makes the best macaroni and cheese I've ever eaten."

Viviana breathed a sigh of relief when the spotlight shifted from her and Noah to family recipes. Along with the other women, she ate and drank too much when the waiters returned to bring out more carafes of libations. They laughed incessantly at anything and everything, and Viviana could not remember when she had felt so free and uninhibited. Even when she'd accompanied her college friends on the birthday cruise, there'd still been the lingering cloud of her financial problems. Now that she had declared bankruptcy and was not responsible for the debts incurred during the theft of her identity, she looked forward to starting over.

Viviana thought of having to shut down her business temporarily as just that: temporary. She was positive that the zoning board would approve converting her property from business to residential, and subsequently she'd be back to business once Noah received the approval to build.

"I'm sorry, my friends, but I'm going to have to go for a walk before I embarrass myself and fall asleep right here," Sandra said.

Lynette stood up. "You're not the only one who has eaten and imbibed too much. I'm going inside to take a nap. I'll see you ladies later on tonight at dinner."

One by one, they left the table, and Noah approached Viviana as she headed toward their villa. "Are you all right?"

Her eyes caressed his face. He was gorgeous. "I'm going inside to get my sunglasses. I need to walk, or I'm going to fall asleep."

"Would you like company?"

She rested a hand on his arm. "Yes."

"I'll get my glasses, too, and we'll walk together."

Noah threaded their fingers together as they walked barefoot along the near-white sand. He'd watched her interact with the wives of his friends who'd attended Yale with him. He didn't know what they were talking about but had to smile to himself when hearing their outbursts of laughter.

He'd met Philip, Brandon, Trace and Richard during their first year at the Ivy League college, and they had become fast friends. He'd invited them to stay with him during school holiday. His friends appeared unaffected by his mother's snobbishness and truly were amazed when their wants and needs were met by the Wainwright household staff.

Noah and his friends invited the prospective groom into what they considered their exclusive circle during their last year. Jerome Tucker had been injured during a hit-and-run in which he'd broken an arm and a leg and was in danger of not completing his senior year. Brandon, who was a business major and in some of the same classes as Jerome, suggested that Noah, who had a car, pick up his classmate from his apartment and drive him to the campus every day.

"Did my friends' wives try to get into your business?"

Viviana smiled. "The only thing I'm going to say is they were very curious about us dating especially since they haven't seen you with a woman in almost two years."

Noah stared at a sand crab making its way into the water as a bird swooped down to have it for a meal. "That's because I haven't dated exclusively for a while."

She glanced up at him. "Why?"

"Because the last woman I dated issued an ultimatum—it was her or my work."

"And you chose work."

He nodded. "It wasn't only work. She felt that because we had been seeing each other for almost six months, she wanted an engagement ring."

"That's rather demanding."

"I felt the same," Noah said in agreement. He stopped and pulled Viviana against his body. "Do you have a time limit for dating or a period of engagement?"

"I've never really thought about it," she said. "But if I were ever to become engaged, I'd prefer a long rather than a short engagement."

"Why?"

She eased back, staring up at him through the lenses of her dark glasses. A breeze off the ocean had stirred the curls falling over her forehead and around her face. "I'd need that length of time to discover if I truly wanted to commit my future to a man who would become my husband and perhaps the father of my children. I've had friends who dated someone, and it was all nice and good because the guys were on their best behavior. But once married, they changed into strangers. It was as if the marriage license had become a sign of ownership. They'd complain to me they felt more like chattel than a partner."

"The signs were probably there before they were married, and they chose to ignore them."

"Maybe you're right, but women tend to love with

their hearts rather than their heads. We liken ourselves to the girls in fairy tales, where the prince is going to come along and take us away and we will live happily ever after."

Noah smiled. "Now that sounds like a romance novel."

Viviana made a fist and punched him softly in the chest. "What's wrong with romance novels? I read them all of the time."

"That's probably why you've been so unlucky in love."

"Why would you say that?"

"Romance novels are based on fantasy, not the real world."

"It's fantasy within the realm of reality, Noah. You can't say some of the situations don't exist."

"I'm not saying that, sweetheart, but the books always end with a happily-ever-after."

"Why are you so cynical?" she asked, frowning. "How long have your parents been married?"

"Forty-two years."

"People don't stay together if they don't love each other. I'm certain your parents may have had their ups and downs, but it has to be more ups because they're still married."

Noah buried his face in Viviana's hair. He knew she was right. The first ten years of his parents' marriage had been tenuous, yet somehow they had decided to stay together. Viviana had accused him of being cynical when he wasn't. It was just that he'd found himself falling in love with her, and he believed it was all for the wrong reason. Not only did he want to take care of her, he also wanted to right all of the wrongs she had experienced with the other men in her life, beginning with her father.

"You're right," Noah said after a pregnant pause. "In the beginning of the marriage, my mother was the stronger of the two and called the shots, but then things changed when she became a grandmother. Now she's a mush, and Dad occasionally will roar like a lion."

He smothered a groan when Viviana pressed her breasts to his chest. Anchoring his hands on the sides of her head, he eased back and covered her mouth with his, ignoring her soft moans as she kissed him back. One minute they were standing upright and the next they were on the sand, his body half-on and half-off hers as he communicated without words how much he wanted her. Not only did he want her in his bed but also in his life. He'd asked her to let him in, and she'd admitted that he was in, but that still was not enough.

Noah did not want Viviana. He craved her. She had become his drug of choice, which he never wanted to give up. Whenever she looked at him, he felt as if she could see what he was thinking, and that alone made him uncomfortable and put him at risk of losing control. All his life, he had prided himself on his iron-willed self-control.

He reversed their position, pulling Viviana atop his body as he continued to devour her mouth like a man deprived of food needed for survival. Noah knew he had lied to himself the first time he saw Viviana and he couldn't pull his gaze away because she unknowingly had bewitched him. He'd known and seen his share of beautiful women all over the world, yet there was something about her that held him spellbound.

Viviana felt Noah's erection pulsing against her middle, and she knew she had to stop him before she begged him to make love to her on the beach where anyone could come along and see them.

"Please stop, Noah!" She must have gotten through to him because he raised his head. Both were still wearing sunglasses so she couldn't see his eyes, but she felt the strong beating of his heart against her breasts. "We can't do this here."

Breathing heavily, he buried his face between her chin and shoulder. "You're right. I'm sorry."

Viviana pressed her fingertips to his mouth. "Don't apologize, darling."

His pale eyebrows lifted. "That's the second time you called me *darling*. Am I your darling?"

She smiled. "You are if you want to be."

"I do."

"If I am your sweetheart, then you are my darling."

He smiled. "What can I expect for the honor?"

Viviana ran a forefinger down the length of his straight nose. "I don't know. Maybe I'll think of something before we go back to the States."

Noah tickled her ribs, and she squirmed to escape his fingers. "Don't! I'm ticklish."

Pressing a kiss under her ear, Noah then nibbled the

lobe. "You shouldn't have told me that because I'm a tickle monster."

Viviana's hand went to his hair, pushing a wave off his tanned forehead. "Do you tickle your nieces and nephews?"

"No. I only have one nephew, and he just turned one."

"Your parents have four children and only one has a child?"

Noah rolled over and stood up and pulled Viviana up with him. "That's a sore spot with my mother. You cannot mention grandchildren around her because she will go into a tizzy. All of her friends have grandchildren, and I believe they're a little catty when they remind her of how many they have. She felt a little better when Jordan and his wife had Maxwell, but for her that's not enough."

"What are you waiting for, Noah?" she teased. "You're the next in line to give your mama a grandbaby."

"When I get a woman pregnant, she will be my wife and not my girlfriend."

Viviana felt as if she'd been verbally slapped for saying the wrong thing. "I think it's time we head back. I want to change into my swimsuit and hang out on the beach before it's time for dinner."

They retraced their steps without holding hands, and she felt a chill growing between them despite the intense heat of the sun beating down on them. Viviana wondered if perhaps Noah had gotten a woman pregnant and she either had not wanted to marry him or had terminated it. If talking about babies was verboten, then she promised herself she would never bring it up again.

Chapter Seven

It was past midnight, and Noah found himself staring up at the ceiling as he lay in bed, his head resting on his folded arms. Not even the sounds of the ocean washing up on the beach or the rustle of palm fronds coming in through the screened windows could lull him to sleep. Jerome and Tasha's wedding was scheduled for later that afternoon, and come Sunday he wanted to know if Viviana was going to accompany him to Emerald Cove or go back to the States.

Jerome, his fiancée, their parents and the wedding party had checked in to one of the larger villas accommodating up to twelve. He didn't get to see Jerome much now that he'd relocated from New Jersey to California to set up his own department with a small, private bank. Once Jerome had proposed to his physician girlfriend, he'd teased Noah about being the last hold-out of the group. What his friends did not know was that he still hadn't found the woman who would get him to change his marital status from single to married. But that had changed when he walked into the historic house in Wickham Falls, West Virginia. He did not know what it was about Viviana Remington, other than her obvious beauty that had him thinking about her when they were hundreds of miles apart. And he wondered also if he wanted to sleep with her only to satisfy his curiosity about her being nothing more than a fixation he needed to assuage. The more he thought about Viviana the more Noah realized he was deluding himself. Even when he was physically so close to her, kissing and touching her, he felt a chasm between them he wasn't able to bridge, and that's when he believed karma was repaying him for dating women and then leaving them once they sought more from him than he was willing to give.

However, there'd been a time, when he was twenty-three, that he'd believed that he had met the woman he wanted to marry, but it soured when he discovered she was cheating on him. And if he hadn't known about the first ten years of his parents' marriage, perhaps he would think differently about asking a woman to be his wife. His father, who, while he was engaged to his mother, had had an affair with another woman that produced a child.

Noah swallowed the lump in his throat. He felt as if he'd lost Viviana, even though she slept in a bed less than fifty feet from his own. After the walk on the beach, she'd become overly polite and distant. She'd returned and changed into a one-piece swimsuit that did little to cool his desire to make love with her.

She had bonded with the wives of his friends and spent most of her time with them. The exception was when everyone gathered in the resort's dining room for meals. They sat next to each other, and whenever her arm brushed his, Noah felt as if he was coming out of his skin. His younger brother had taken up yoga to relax, and Noah wished he had taken Rhett's advice and joined his classes.

Knowing he wasn't going to sleep, Noah sat up and tossed back the sheet. He found a pair of shorts and slipped them on. Walking barefoot, he unlocked the screen door and walked out into the night. He saw something out of the corner of his eye and spied someone sitting on the beach. A full moon lit up the night, and as he made his way down to the water, he couldn't stop smiling.

She glanced up at him and smiled. "It looks as if I'm not the only one who couldn't sleep."

Noah sank down next to her on the damp sand. Even in the eerie light, he could discern that the sun had darkened her skin to a deep mahogany. "I've never been much of an insomniac before meeting you."

Viviana pulled her legs up to her chest and wrapped her arms around her knees. "I'm not going to accept blame for that."

"Can you accept that I'm falling in love with you?"

Her head turned toward him slowly, and she looked

as if she was going to jump up and run away. "Please don't say that, Noah."

"And why shouldn't I say it, Viviana?"

"Because you don't know what you're saying. You don't know me, and I certainly don't know you."

He reached for her, and then pulled back when she glared at him. She turned away and stared out at the incoming tide. She was so still that she could have been carved from marble.

"What do you think your rich and powerful family would say if you decided to bring home the daughter of a man who neglected his family because he loved drugs more than he loved them? That he spent five years in prison for armed robbery to get enough money to pay his dealer? He wasn't even there when my mother lay dying and calling out his name. I'd just turned seven when my father came to my mother's funeral in handcuffs and leg-irons. The marshals with him wouldn't let him sit with me and Lee or go up to the casket so he could see her one last time. The scene haunted me for years, and every time I saw a little girl with her father, I wanted to change places with her."

"Have you forgiven your father?"

"I did, once I was older."

"Then, why are you agonizing over something that's in the past, sweetheart? Your father isn't the only person that's had to seek redemption."

She turned to look at him. "Your father went to prison?"

Noah smiled. "No. But what he did to my mother was a lot worse." He knew he had to tell Viviana something he'd never told a woman outside of his family. "My father was engaged to my mother when he slept with another woman and got her pregnant. My grandfather and the girl's father concocted a scheme that, when she had the child, the baby's birth certificate would list Christiane Johnston as the mother's name and Edward Lincoln Wainwright as the father." He ignored Viviane's audible gasp. "My mother was forced to raise another woman's child as her own. My parents stayed married but did not share a bed for almost ten years. That's why there's a decade between me and my older brother."

"Did she treat him differently than she did her other children?"

"No. She claims the moment she held Jordan she became his mother. There are times when I believe she loves him more than she loves me, Rhett and Chanel. After all, he was her only child for a long time. And now that he's made her a grandmother, she's over the moon."

"When did you find out about your father's affair?"

"I was still in college when Jordan told me that he'd overheard our father and grandfather arguing. I think it was the first time my father had challenged his father. Jordan was devastated to know what they'd done to our mother. It took years before he, Dad and Grandpa declared a truce. Jordan did get to meet his biological mother, who'd married and had two daughters. His half sisters were bridal attendants in his wedding. I know what went on in my family cannot begin to compare with you growing up with a drug-addicted father who wasn't there for you. It had to be traumatizing for you as a child."

Viviana brushed grains of sand off her bare legs. "Your family was able to bury its secret, while my mother's family's sins are an open book. The Wolfes are mentioned in social-studies books under listings as the most corrupt, worst mine owners in West Virginia's history."

Noah moved closer and rubbed her back in a comforting gesture. He felt her stiffen before relaxing against his palm. "How long do you intend to carry the sins of your ancestors?"

"It's not me but the folks in The Falls that refuse to let me forget. People have called me that junkie's or that jailbird's daughter to my face. It took a long time for me to ignore them as mean or ignorant. Even to this day I don't socialize with a lot people in town. And then there's the time when Leland was falsely accused of breaking into a house, and everyone was quick to judge him because my father was in jail serving time for armed robbery."

"I know it's easy for me to say the hell with them because I haven't experienced what you've had to go through. The only thing you should be concerned with is treating folks fairly so they'll refer others while coming back again and again."

"That's what I'm hoping, Noah. Running a B and B is different from a boardinghouse because I never lacked for boarders who were single men on a fixed income and needed a roof over their heads."

"Don't forget you live in a town with small businesses that definitely rely on word-of-mouth and referrals to get customers. It will probably be the same with your B and B."

Viviana nodded. "You're right. It's just that I have to try and convince myself."

Noah pulled her closer. "I'll remind you whenever you forget."

She rested her head on his shoulder "Do you know that you're good for me?"

"I sort of suspected that, but I was waiting for you to tell me."

"Have you no modesty?" Viviana asked. There was a hint of laughter in her voice.

"Nope. Modesty isn't a part of my personality."

Viviana uncrossed her legs. "It's time I go back and get ready for bed."

Noah stood and extended his hand to help her to her feet. "Do you need help going to sleep?"

Viviana rested her hands on his bare chest. "I just might. Give me about fifteen minutes to shower and get into bed before you come over. Nothing can happen for a few days because it's my time of the month."

Noah pressed a kiss to her forehead. "Not to worry. Remember, I said you have to come to me and not the other way around."

She curved an arm around his waist as they headed back to the villas. "I do remember that."

Noah left Viviana at her door, waiting until she locked it behind her before walking into his suite. He took a quick shower to wash the sand off his body. When he did open the door to the adjoining suite, he encountered darkness except for the light Viviana had

left on in the bathroom. He slipped into bed next to
her, smiling when she turned to face him and draped
an arm over his neck.

"What took you so long?" she crooned against his
mouth.

"I had to take another shower to get rid of the sand."

Viviana looped a bare leg over his pajama-covered
one. "I can't believe the places where grains of sand
seem to hide."

Her mint-scented breath mingling with the fragrance of flowers on her hair and body wafted into his.

He lay still, listening for the change in her breathing that indicated she had fallen asleep, and this time
Morpheus was kinder to him when he fell into a deep,
comforting sleep.

Noah did not want to believe Viviana could improve
on perfection, yet she had. She had parted her hair in
the middle, and it hung straight down her back to her
waist. The vermilion color on her lips matched her
manicured nails and toes. When she spun around on
the toes of her black stilettos, the flowing skirt of the
matching lace halter dress showed off her long brown
legs. The bodice was low enough to reveal a hint of
firm breasts each time she inhaled.

He stared at the smoky shadow on her lids that made
her brown eyes appear even lighter.

"You look incredible." He was unable to conceal
the awe in his voice.

She executed a graceful curtsy. "Thank you."

Closing the distance between them, he ran his

hand over her silken hair. "What did you do with your curls?"

Viviana smiled up at him. "They're still there. I just used a flat iron to straighten them."

"I like your curly hair." He took her hands, staring at the bracelets on her wrists. The colorful beads and the intricate workmanship was exquisite, reminding him of pieces he'd seen in museums. "I've never seen you wear these."

"My father made them for me. The one on my right wrist represents his Native American bloodline, and the one on the left is for his African American ancestry. He gave them to me for my twenty-eighth birthday."

"He's very talented."

Viviana nodded. "I agree. But then I'm biased because he's my dad."

Noah continued to stare at her, his eyes caressing her face. When he'd woken up in bed with her earlier that morning, Noah knew it was something he wanted to repeat over and over when he saw her mussed hair flowing over the pillow and heard the husky timbre of her voice when she greeted him with a shy smile. He had to admit that he'd slept more soundly than he had in weeks. He'd suggested they order room service, and when she'd agreed, he returned to his suite to allow her the privacy she needed to complete her morning ablution.

After eating, they went back to bed and just lay there not talking, but somehow they'd managed to communicate without saying a word. They were content to enjoy the other's warmth and companionship.

Noah was more than aware of her fragility and knew he had to be patient with Viviana. She had taken hits from not only her townsfolk but also from men who sensed she was an easy mark and used it to their best advantage. He had to convince her that there wasn't anything he wanted from her except love. He'd stripped himself bare when he admitted he was falling in love with her, and he knew he would have to wait for her to trust him enough to offer him her love.

"I think it's time we leave, or we're going to miss the ceremony." Reaching for his jacket, he slipped his arm into the sleeves. In recognition of the weather, ties were not required. Noah waited for Viviana to pick up a small black evening bag with a narrow shoulder strap and then extended his hand to lead her outside and down the beach to where tents had been set up for the wedding ceremony and the reception to follow.

Viviana held Noah's hand throughout the entire ceremony as Jerome Tucker exchanged vows with Dr. Tasha Clarkson. She gave him a furtive glance, wondering what was going on behind his impassive expression as he sat staring straight ahead.

The bride appeared ethereal in a Grecian-styled white gown in flowing organza that reminded Viviana of peaks of frothy cream. She had pinned tiny white flowers into the thick coil of hair on her nape in lieu of a veil. Her sisters were her attendants, and they wore one-shouldered gowns in varying shades of pink. Jerome had selected his father to be his best man and younger brothers at his groomsmen.

The resort's wedding planner had had her staff set up baskets of flowers along both sides of the white carpet leading to the beach and attach pink ribbons to the chairs set up theater-style under the tent. Viviana liked the idea of a destination wedding because of its simplicity. Yes, she thought, if she did marry, then she would want a destination wedding with the beach as the venue and reception hall.

Jerome and Tasha sealed their vows with a long, drawn-out kiss amid whistling and rousing applause. Viviana smiled at Noah when he raised their clasped hands and kissed the back of hers. His eyes were darker, mysterious, and she wondered if he was imagining their wedding day.

Sitting on the beach in the moonlight had been a time for confessions and revelations. He'd admitted he loved her, and she had bared her soul about her childhood. He had disclosed the circumstances behind his father's infidelity, while she poured out her heart about always feeling like a resident alien in her own hometown.

Viviana knew she was falling in love with Noah yet was loath to tell him. Each and every time she'd told a man she loved him, it had resulted in a broken heart.

She and Noah rose to stand with the assembly as Jerome and Tasha processed down the carpet, each stopping to greet their guests. Jerome pumped Noah's hand like a politician campaigning for office, then whispered in his ear and at the same time winked at her.

"What did he tell you?" she asked Noah.

He pressed his mouth to her ear. "He said he's going to come for me if I let you get away."

Viviana met his eyes. "He'll have to make good on that warning if you break my heart."

Noah's right hand moved down her bare back and rested on her hip. "I promise that's never going to happen, sweetheart."

She was unsuccessful at concealing the shudder racing along her nerve endings as Noah's fingers caressed her exposed skin. "Don't make promises you can't keep, Noah."

"This is one I intend to keep."

Viviana did not want to debate the issue with him. She'd had enough verbal confrontations with her exes to last her several lifetimes. She was the first to admit she was generous and much too trusting, but she was also a survivor. She survived losing her mother, and not having her father around when growing up, facing alienation from townspeople because she was a descendant of the Wolfes, and her failed relationships. When compared to the residents in The Falls, she had grown up privileged and protected. She had had the support of her aunt who had enrolled her and Leland in a private school thirty miles from Wickham Falls to protect them from the taunts from children that repeated what they'd overheard from their parents.

"Noah," she whispered.

"What is it, babe?"

"Do you realize you're feeling me up in public?"

His hand stilled. "Is that what I'm doing?"

Reaching around her back, she placed her hand over his. "Don't play the innocent, darling."

Noah chuckled softly. "I'm practicing for the time when you'll let me touch and taste every inch of your delicious-looking body."

The heat in her face had nothing to do with the intense sunlight outside the protective cover of the white tent. She smiled and demurely lowered her eyes. "You may not have to wait too much longer."

"What are you saying?"

"When we get to Emerald Cove…" Her words were preempted when Noah's mouth covered hers in an explosive kiss that robbed her lungs of oxygen.

"You two need to get a room," said a deep male voice.

Viviana and Noah sprang apart like kids caught at something they weren't supposed to do. "We have a room," Noah said, smiling.

Alicia and Brandon were grinning from ear to ear. "Look at you, guys," she drawled. "You should be in *People* magazine's most beautiful couples."

Viviana had to admit Noah looked like a male model with his sun-bleached hair and sun-browned face and body. The pale gray tailored linen suit, banded-collar untucked white shirt and black imported loafers enhanced his overall good looks. It hadn't taken her long to overcome her aversion to blond men.

Noah splayed his fingers under Viviana's hair on her bared back. "Viviana is the one who would definitely make the cut as the most beautiful."

Alicia tightened her hold on Brandon's arm. Stunning in a strapless floral print gown with a flowing skirt, she had styled her braided hair in a messy bun on the nape of her neck. "Now I know why you and Brandon are friends. You both know what to say to flatter your women."

Brandon smiled at his wife. "We only speak the truth and nothing but the truth."

Viviana and Alicia shared a smile when the two men executed a fist bump. Minutes later, they were joined by Lynette, Michelle and Sandra and their husbands. "Now that the gang's all here, I think it's time we put some life into this part-tee."

Alicia rolled her eyes at Brandon. "If you even attempt to pretend you guys are a boy band, I'll divorce you."

"Start drawing up the papers," Trace said, "because Jerome is joining us when we lip-synch to the Backstreet Boys and New Edition."

Viviana stared up at Noah. "He's kidding, isn't he?"

Lynette shook her head. "No, he isn't. These old fools didn't join a fraternity, so they decided they were a boy band and couldn't wait for a function to become part of the entertainment."

Noah winked at Lynette. "You have to admit that we do have some smooth moves."

"Yeah, right," Michelle drawled under her breath.

"We've been practicing when you ladies weren't looking," Philip said.

As a newcomer to the group of friends, Viviana couldn't wait to see them perform. One of two photographers came over and snapped photos of the couples as Viviana leaned closer to Noah. There was one shot when she smiled up at him smiling down at her, unaware that the love she felt for him was reflected in her eyes and in her smile.

A sumptuous dinner followed the cocktail hour with a DJ spinning old and new tunes that had many of the guests singing along or moving in their chairs. Jerome walked to the portable floor that had been set up for dancing and picked up a handheld microphone. He'd shed his tuxedo jacket. Viviana was awed by his resemblance to the actor Morris Chestnut.

"Tasha and I would like to thank everyone who traveled from afar to help us celebrate this momentous occasion. Even though I have biological brothers, there are a few other guys who've been like brothers to me. And for those who don't know who they are, I'd like Philip, Brandon, Noah and Trace to stand and come up to the stage. I've always said that if we ever fell on hard times, we could hire ourselves out as wedding singers. Hold up, folks," he said when there was laughter from the assembly. "After we perform, I promise not to pass the plate."

Viviana clasped her hands tightly as she watched the four men take off their jackets and join Jerome on the stage. He gave the DJ the mike and stood in front of the others, their hands behind their backs. She smiled when she recognized the opening bars to the Backstreet Boys' "I Want It That Way."

She stopped herself from jumping up and applauding when they lip-synched to the classic hit, using folding chairs as props during their choreography. The song ended with stunned silence before everyone was up on their feet cheering and whistling. The applause hadn't faded away when the quintet launched into one of her all-time favorites—"Can You Stand the Rain" by New Edition. She'd watched the movie *The Best Man Holiday* over and over because of the dance sequence. She did scream when Noah pointed at her and mouthed along. It was obvious they had been practicing because their choreography was spot-on. The five linked arms and bowed as women screamed and a few threw bills onto the stage. They returned to their tables and were greeted with hugs and kisses from their wives.

Viviana wrapped her arms around Noah's neck and kissed him soundly on the mouth. "You were incredible."

Attractive lines fanned out around his brilliant blue-green eyes. "I told you we had smooth moves."

"Yes, you did. You guys are good."

The DJ put on an upbeat dance number, and Noah cupped her elbow. "Dance with me, sweetheart."

Viviana danced with Noah and seemingly every man in attendance as she lost herself in the nonstop revelry that went on as the sun sank lower in the sky until it was a large orange ball floating above the horizon. After her second drink, she felt slightly lightheaded and changed her beverage choice to sparkling water with a twist of lime. She didn't see Noah for about twenty minutes, and when he returned, he pulled her toward an area where he could talk to her without shouting.

"I made arrangements for us to leave here tomorrow after breakfast. We'll be taking a catamaran over to Emerald Cove."

Viviana nodded. "I'll make certain to pack tonight."

"How long do you want to stay?"

"Oh. I have a choice?"

He angled his head. "You will always a choice with me."

"A week."

"That's all?"

"You want to stay longer?" she asked.

"I'll stay as long as you want. We just have to be back in the States in time for Thanksgiving. I can't wait for you to meet my family."

"That's not possible, Noah."

He frowned. "Why not?"

"Because I promised my brother that I would spend Thanksgiving with him and his family."

"What about Christmas and New Year's?"

"I'm going to Arizona to see my aunt and uncle." Viviana could tell by Noah's dour expression that he wasn't too happy about the plans she had for the holidays, but she had no intention of changing them. Not only was her immediate family small, but they also lived in different states. "Maybe next year. And it's much too soon to meet your family because by that time we'll only have been dating a couple of weeks."

"Yeah. Maybe next year."

"Why do you say it like that, Noah?"

"Say what?"

"Like you're upset. I only have Lee—and now Angela

and their twins—and my aunt and uncle as family, while you have a hoard of Wainwrights. The Wolfes would have ceased to exist if Lee and Angela had decided not to have any children together."

Noah cupped her neck in his hands. "What about you, Viv? Don't you want children?"

"I've never thought much about it," she said truthfully.

"And why not?"

"Because I've had so much piss-poor luck with men that it isn't something I think about. And there's no way I want to bring a child into a situation where his or her mother and father are always at each other's throats. I come from a broken home, and that's not something I'd want for my kids. I know there are situations like Angela losing her husband in combat and being left with two children to raise on her own, but that's the exception. Even though my parents were married, it still wasn't a stable home."

"No marriage is without its ups and downs."

Viviana did not know if Noah loved her enough to propose marriage, but she wasn't about to fall into his arms and confess her undying love and have him do something to break her heart and force her to turn from relationships forever.

"I think of your mother as a martyr for accepting her husband's love child when he hadn't given her one of her own. What if the situation were reversed? Do you think your father would've married your mother if he knew his fiancée was sleeping with another man and found herself pregnant with his child?" She held up a hand when he opened his mouth. "The answer is a re-sounding *no* because of pride. The fact that the other woman was carrying a Wainwright made all of the dif-ference. Did you stop to think that maybe I wouldn't want to marry you just because I was pregnant?"

His fingers moved up and held her head. "Of course we would discuss it."

"Really, Noah. What if I told you I wouldn't marry you until after the baby's birth?"

His eyes grew cold, forbidding. "Then, I suppose I'd have to wait."

"You'd wait because I wouldn't give you a choice. By the way, did your investigator tell you that my mother was engaged to another man when she found herself pregnant by my father?"

"No."

"So you see, it's the reverse of what happened to you parents. My mother broke her engagement to a boy from a well-to-do family and married Emory but lost the baby when she fell down a flight of stairs. My grandparents hated my father because he was poor and mixed-race. So he had two strikes against him, but they accepted me and Lee because we carried Wolfe blood."

"My brother Jordan's biological mother is black, so the Wolfes aren't the only family with mixed-race progeny. My cousin Brandt is married to an African American woman, and it is obvious Mya is also mixed-race, so you mentioning race is nothing more than BS."

"I didn't mention race because…"

"Because what?" Noah asked when her words trailed off. "I happen to have perfect vision, so I know you have mixed ancestry, but that means absolutely nothing when it comes to how I feel about you. So, let this be the last time we discuss this."

Viviana wanted to remind Noah that he was moving much too fast, that he was attempting to fast-forward their relationship by wanting to introduce her to his family.

Chapter Eight

"Welcome back, Mr. Wainwright."

Noah greeted the man who'd met them at the pier with a warm smile and handshake. "Thank you, Mr. Lawrence." All of the employees at Emerald Cove addressed one another and guests by their last names. "How is the family?"

"They're well, thank you." The slight-built dark-skinned man opened the door of the jitney for Noah to help Viviana in and then placed their bags in the compartment behind the rear seats.

Noah gave Viviana a sidelong glance. They hadn't shared a bed following the wedding, each retreating to their own suite. She'd offered her cheek instead of her lips for a good-night kiss, and he knew she was still miffed because of their conversation about marriage and babies. He knew she was reluctant to even consider sharing her life and future with him, whereas he was willing to put a ring on her finger and then agree to a long engagement, if that was what she wanted. What Noah did not want to consider was losing her.

Noah realized he had to change; he had to stop thinking of only what he wanted and about what Viviana wanted and needed because he was cognizant of what she had gone through with past relationships. Men had used and abused her emotionally, while he'd found himself attempting to bend her to his will and do his bidding.

What she didn't know was that he had tired of the merry-go-round of women a long time ago but feared getting off the ride because he might not find *the one*— the one woman who could make him slow down and stop looking for the next thrill. It had taken him a while to realize he was an adrenaline junkie when he had flown to Spain to view the bullfights or driven from there to Le Mans, France, to attend the 24 Heures du Mans. He'd alternated visiting Venice and Rio for Carnival, and one year he'd attended the one in Trinidad and fallen in love with the island, its food and the women. He'd extended his stay for several months and returned to the States exhausted and thinner than when he'd left due to lack of sleep. He'd left the States weighing 215 and returned at 170 pounds stretched over his six-two frame.

Noah realized he hurt his mother most when she cried at the sight of his gaunt appearance, and he swore he wouldn't do again. It had ended when his father had sat him down and told him that he was preparing to retire as CEO, and it was time for him to step up because Jordan had sworn never to work for WDG.

"Fasten your seat belt, sweetheart," Noah said to Viviana. "The road is a little uneven until we get closer to the resort."

She secured her belt. "If you own the island, then why don't you pave the road?"

"Several roads are bridle paths for those wishing to go horseback riding."

"You have horses on the island?"

"Yes. Horses, pigs, chickens, cows, goats and sheep."

She smiled. "It sounds like a regular Old Mac-Donald's farm."

"The chefs raise and butcher their own meat on the premises. They also grow most of the vegetables in what they call *farm-to-table*."

"That's very convenient."

"It is," Noah agreed. "It saves flying foodstuff in from other islands or as far away as Nassau."

Viviana placed her hand on his, and when he turned it over, they laced their fingers. It was the first display of affection she'd shown him since kissing him after the lip-synch performance. Noah knew he had to be very patient with Viviana and not put undue pressure on her to come to love him as much as he was beginning to love her.

He could not imagine what she'd experienced as a child. Not only had she faced alienation through no fault of her own from people she'd known all of her life, but her grandparents had also rejected her father because of his ancestry. Rejection, alienation, loss and abandonment had followed her like the plague, dragging her down to the point that she gravitated to anyone who showed her a modicum of kindness.

"Who cares for the animals?"

Her query broke into his musings. "We have a veterinary assistant on staff. Whenever a dam or heifer is close to giving birth, a vet from the mainland is flown in to assist with the birthing. I must admit the first time I saw calf being born, I nearly lost the contents of my stomach."

"That's because you're a city boy," Viviana teased. "I went to college with a girl who grew up on a farm, and when I went to visit her, we'd get up early and go to the henhouse to gather eggs. I wore boots and carried a stick to beat the ground to chase away snakes that may have gotten in to steal the eggs."

"Did you ever see a snake?"

"Yes, a few times."

"Were you afraid?" Noah asked her.

"Heck no. I was taught which ones are poisonous. The Falls is surrounded by woods and forests with deer, fox, snakes, bats, coyote, opossum, hawks and eagles."

"What about bears?"

"Bears, wolves and beaver aren't very common anymore."

"Did you go hunting?"

Viviana shook her head. "No. Some families back home live on deer meat all winter."

Noah noticed Viviana referred to Wickham Falls as *home* and wondered if she would ever consider relocating in the future. Her aunt had moved to Arizona, her brother who'd joined the military now lived in North Carolina, and despite all she'd experienced, she had stayed.

He pointed to his left. "There's someone on a horse." Sunlight glinted off the stallion's coal-black coat as it galloped along the trail.

Viviana leaned forward. "What a beautiful animal."

The rutted road gave way to a smooth paved surface, and the driver accelerated, passing dozens of Bahamian-style homes facing the ocean, and coming to a stop near a group of guesthouses constructed over the water. He unloaded the bags from the jitney and left them near the door at the far end of the walkway.

Noah smiled when he saw Viviana, with wide eyes, stare at the white stucco buildings with red-tiled roofs that appeared to be floating on the ocean. "Come on, sweetheart. Let's get you settled in before I take you on a tour."

Viviana followed Noah along the walkway overlooking an infinity pool that separated connecting buildings. He tapped several buttons on a keypad and pushed open the door. The interior, with an open floor plan, belied the compact-looking exterior due to its floor-to-ceiling windows and pocket doors. The kitchen opened up to the family room, making for easier flow for entertaining. Everything reflected a comfortable, relaxed feeling that pulled her invitingly to stay awhile.

She turned to find Noah with his arms crossed over his chest. "It's beautiful."

He smiled. "I'm glad you like it."

"Is this one mine?"

"Do you want it?"

Viviana strolled into the dining room and ran her fingertips over the fabric of classic Chippendale-style dining chairs. The chairs were similar to those in the dining room of the bed-and-breakfast. If her brother hadn't paid the delinquent property taxes, she would've been forced to sell off many of the authentic antiques in the house.

She walked over to Noah and wrapped her arms around his waist. "Yes."

He rested his chin on the top of her head. "Then, it's yours."

Viviana leaned back and met eyes that were filled with laughter. "Where are you going to stay?"

"There's a door in the kitchen that connects this guesthouse to mine."

She knew it was just a matter of time before she and Noah would share a bed again, and it wouldn't be only to sleep but to make love. "Do you know what I'd like to do?"

Noah cradled her face in his hands. "What's that?"

"I'd like to spend the rest of the day with you right here."

"You don't want to see the resort?"

Viviana shook her head. "Not today. I want to swim laps in the infinity pool, and then lie out, soaking up the sun until I'm well-done."

"You're already well-done. I can't see your freckles anymore." Noah kissed the end of her nose. "Let me know what you want to eat for dinner, and I'll call the chef and place an order."

A slight frown appeared between her eyes. "Why do you have a kitchen if you don't use it?"

"I'd use it if I could cook."

"What if I teach you to cook?"

"You're kidding, aren't you?"

Viviana saw a slight hesitation in Noah's eyes, and it was the first time since meeting him that he didn't appear the overly confident, cocky young man who was used to getting what he wanted just by picking up a phone. "No, I'm not kidding, Noah. You can't go through life expecting someone to feed you. What if you were stranded and had to fend for yourself? How would you expect to survive?"

Bending slightly, Noah scooped her up in his arms and spun her around and around. "I'd call a local restaurant and have Grubhub deliver my order."

Viviana scrunched up her nose. "You're impossible. Now, please put me down."

He set her on her feet. "I'm willing to be your student for three lessons."

"Five."

"Four and no more, sweetheart."

Going on tiptoe, she pressed a kiss over one of his eyes. "That's one." She kissed his other eye. "Two." The bridge of his nose. "Three." And then his mouth. "That's four."

"I think I'm going to enjoy cooking with you. And what's going to make it fun is that I get to flirt with my teacher. I'm going to get your bags so you can change, and I'll do the same."

"Are you falling asleep on me, Viv?"

"I don't think so."

Noah had invited Viviana to share the webbed recliner in the loggia at the rear of his guesthouse. They'd spent the day swimming laps in the pool, walking hand in hand along the beach, before returning to the house to shower and change, then ordering room service.

He closed his eyes, and suddenly all of his senses were magnified: the warmth of Viviana's body; the silken feel of her smooth skin; the hypnotic scent of the perfumed crème she'd put on after her shower; and the soft whisper of her even breathing. Noah shifted her body as he sat up.

"I'm going to take you to bed."

Viviana opened her eyes and smiled. "I'm not sleepy."

"If you're not sleepy, then what are you?"

"I was just resting my eyes."

Noah lifted her effortlessly. "You can rest your eyes in your own bed."

Viviana put her arms around his neck and laid her head on his shoulder. After spending several days with her, he'd discovered she wasn't much of a drinker. He'd ordered a bottle of wine with their dinner, and she'd drunk half a glass before setting it aside.

His urgent need to make love to her had waned once he realized he would spend more than six days with her. Noah didn't know how long they would remain at

Emerald Cove, but he planned to take it one day at a time and enjoy every second, minute, hour, day or week with Viviana Remington. Walking into her bedroom, he placed her on the bed and pulled up the sheet and a lightweight blanket over her shoulders.

Noah dimmed the lamp to the lowest setting on the bedside table, adjusted the thermostat and walked out of the bedroom, closing the door behind him. He sat on a chair outside the pool, and minutes later his cell phone chimed a familiar ringtone he'd programmed for his older brother.

"What's up, Jordan?"

"I've been trying to call you for days and kept getting a message that your mailbox is full."

"It's not full. Cell phone reception is spotty here."

"Where have you been?"

"I'm down here in the Bahamas. I had to go to a friend's wedding. Right now I'm on Emerald Cove. Why have you been calling me?"

"Mom told me it's your turn to choose the charity for the New Year's Eve fund-raiser. She's panicking because the printer told her he can't send out the invitations until he gets the name of the earmarked charity."

"Wounded Warrior Project." It was the first thing that popped into Noah's head.

"Excellent choice. I'm certain this would make Giles happy because he's still in contact with a lot of guys in the corps. Thanks, bro. I'm going to call Mom and tell her."

"Wait, Jordan. I need to talk to you about something."

There came a beat. "What's wrong, Noah?"

He heard the concern in Jordan's voice. "Nothing's wrong. It's... Who am I kidding?" Noah said. "I have a dilemma."

"Not you!"

"I'm serious, Jordan."

"I'm sorry. Talk to me, brother."

Noah paused, choosing his words carefully. "How did you know the first time you met her that Aziza was the woman you wanted to marry?"

"I wasn't certain about marrying her, but I knew when I met her that she was someone I wanted to get to know better, even though Brandt had asked me to talk to her about a sexual harassment problem she'd had with her former boss. Her stunning beauty aside, we clicked because we are lawyers, so we had a lot in common. And then, once we began dating, I knew I wanted her to be the last woman in my life. Does this answer your question?"

"Yes and no."

"Don't tell me you've met someone that will make you turn in your bachelor card."

Noah smiled. "I have. Unlike you, the instant I saw Viviana I knew she was the one."

"Wow!"

"Yes, wow. She's the first woman I've known that I want to take care of." Noah gave Jordan a cursory overview of Viviana's failed relationships with other men.

"Has she asked you to take care of her, Noah?"

"No."

"What she needs is for you to love and protect her. Women are a lot stronger than we give them credit for," Jordan said. "I knew I wanted to marry Zee even before I slept with her."

Noah smiled for the first time since answering the call. "Viviana and I haven't made love, and I still want to marry her."

"How long have you known this girl?"

"I met her early August."

"Where does she live?"

"Wickham Falls, West Virginia."

"Damn, Noah! What's up with these West Virginia women? First Giles, and now you."

Noah smiled. "What can I say? We have exquisite taste in women."

"Is she as beautiful as Mya?"

"They have a different type of beauty." Noah thought of Viviana's beauty as sensually dark and smoldering.

"When will the family get to meet her?"

"I don't know. She has prior plans for Thanksgiving and Christmas."

"Bummer. The only advice I'm going to give you is to be patient. From what you've told me, she's been through a lot, and just because you've become her knight in shining armor, it's not going to magically erase her past."

Noah nodded even though Jordan couldn't see him. He'd purposefully not mentioned what Viviana and her brother had had to go through from the residents of Wickham Falls because he didn't want to depict her as a fragile, broken spirit. "There are times when I believe I'm being paid back for the number of women I've dated over the years."

"Did you take advantage of them, Noah?"

"No. At least, I don't believe I did. I took them out, gave them whatever they wanted within reason, and when we broke up, it was never ugly."

"Then, you shouldn't be harboring any guilt."

"I wasn't what I'd consider a love-and-leave-them dude. I equate making love with a woman as a form of commitment. And that means I'm all in, when it comes to our relationship."

"Are you all in with Viviana?"

"Yes."

"Where is she now?"

"She's here with me."

"Emerald Cove is where Zee and I honeymooned, and where I got her pregnant, so be careful, little brother, that you don't get carried away and make a little Wainwright. Mom has been harassing me about giving her another grandchild."

"I heard her sing the same tune when I came up for Dad's birthday. She's not going to get a grandchild from me until I'm married, so she should set her sights on Rhett or Chanel."

"I doubt if that's going to happen, now that they're involved with WDG. Dad said they're like kids running amok in a candy shop. They come in early and stay late in an attempt to learn everything they need to know about real estate."

"That's because it's new to them. Tell our sister and brother to slow down, or they'll burn out before they're thirty."

"I will, whenever I see them again. I'm going to hang up now and call Mom with your charity."

"Give her my love."

"I will. By the way, when are you coming back?"

"I don't know. I'm hoping we can spend a couple of weeks here before heading back to the States. Tell Dad I'll call him to give him enough time to schedule the jet to take us back."

"Okay. Talk to you later, brother."

"Love you, Jordan."

"Love you, too."

Noah ended the call and set the phone on the chair. Talking to Jordan had helped him to see things more clearly when it came to Viviana. He knew he was rushing things because he feared losing her. She'd admitted loving with her heart rather than her head, and for him it was the reverse. He'd never allowed his heart to dictate the terms of any relationship he'd had with a woman—until now.

He sat watching the sun sink lower and lower until it disappeared completely. The night sky was dotted with millions of stars that resembled a sprinkling of diamond dust on black velvet. Noah finally got up and went inside. He closed and locked the pocket doors and walked through Viviana's suite to his own rather than going around to the rear of the connecting guesthouses.

Shock assailed him when he entered his bedroom and found Viviana sitting up in bed waiting for him. Unbound black curls spilled over her forehead and around her shoulders in sensual disarray as she held the sheet over her chest. He swallowed, having realized she was naked under the sheet.

A mysterious smile parted her lips. "What took you so long?"

"I was talking to my brother."

Viviana, still holding the sheet, patted the mattress with her free hand. "Did you mention me?"

"Yes, I did," he admitted as he crossed the room and sat down on the side of the bed. Noah went completely still when Viviana let go of the sheet, wrapped her arms around his body and pressed her naked breasts against his upper arm.

"Was it good?" she whispered.

Noah nodded because at that moment he wasn't able to form any words to speak. "Um, yeah," he managed to get out, moments before her hand searched under his T-shirt to cover his chest, her fingertips caressing his nipples until they were hard as pebbles. He didn't want to believe she was seducing him, when it had been what he'd wanted to do to her for months.

Viviana had no inkling of how many sleepless nights she'd been responsible for when he'd fantasized about making love with her. There were a few nights when he'd woken drenched in sweat and embarrassed that he'd had a nocturnal emission—something he hadn't experienced since coming into puberty at thirteen. And if she didn't stop feeling him up, Noah feared he was going to ejaculate prematurely.

Noah forcibly removed her arms and stood up. He held her gaze as he divested himself of his clothes, smiling when her lips parted and she gasped at seeing that he was fully aroused. Her eyes followed his every move as he opened the drawer in the bedside table and removed a condom. He forced himself to go slow as he slipped the latex sheath over his erection. He had waited months for her, and Noah was willing to wait to give Viviana pleasure before taking his own.

The mattress dipped under his weight when he got into bed with her. Resting both hands on her shoulders, he eased her down. "I won't do anything you don't want me to do."

Smiling and staring up at him under lowered lids, Viviana cradled his face between her palms. "Do whatever you want, but don't break my heart."

Noah lowered his body, supporting his greater weight on his forearms. "I promise never to break your heart."

She placed her fingers over his mouth. "Don't promise. Just don't do it."

Chapter Nine

Noah became an explorer, his mouth and hands charting every dip and curve of Viviana's body. Her soft moans served to heighten his need to possess not only her body but all of her in and out of bed. He had fallen in love with and wanted her to become the last woman in his life.

Nothing in his life mattered except the woman writhing under him. There were a lot of things he'd wanted or craved, but none could come close to the woman in whose scented arms he lay. He eased his erection inside her, meeting a slight resistance before he was fully sheathed inside her. Splaying both hands under her hips, he lifted her higher as he began a slow, measured rhythm.

Viviana bit down on her lip to keep from screaming out the ecstasy she had never experienced with the other men in her past. When Noah had suckled her breasts, she felt as if a part of her had taken flight and left her floating beyond herself. He had taken his time arousing her until she wanted to beg him to take her but also didn't want it to be over. She'd wanted the pleasure to continue until the memory of every man who'd come into her life and used her was eradicated, like an erased chalkboard.

She had stopped asking herself why Noah Wainwright had come into her life like the silent paws of a stalking cat, and when she glanced up, he was there staring at her with large blue-green eyes that had held her in a spell from which she hadn't wanted to escape even if she could have. Viviana had lied to herself over and over that she did not find blond men attractive, yet the blond who was making the most exquisite love to her had proven her wrong.

She exhaled an audible gasp when she felt the first ripple of an orgasm, and she struggled not to climax. Her breathing quickened as she dug her nails in Noah's back. "Oh! Oh! Oh!" she breathed out, over and over.

"Let it go, baby," Noah rasped in her ear. "Please!"

Viviana knew he was as close to climaxing as she was and surrendered to the ecstasy that shattered her into a million little pieces as Noah's groans echoed in her ear and he ground his hips into hers. In between sanity and insanity, they'd ceased to exist as separate entities and become one with the other.

"I love you. I love you," she repeated over and over like a litany. Noah's response to her admission that she loved him was a deep moan as she felt the strong pumping beats of his heart against her breasts.

His head popped up, and he reached over to turn on the bedside lamp. His face was flushed and his eyes a deep moss-green as his chest rose and fell as if he'd run a long, grueling race. A slow smile parted his lips. "Thank you so much for loving me."

Viviana traced a sun-bleached eyebrow with her forefinger. "There's no need to thank me. I tried to convince myself that I didn't want to fall in love with you because I did not want to be hurt again. But somehow you managed to convince me it would be okay."

He pulled out of her body and kissed her forehead. "It wasn't my intent to convince you, but I'm glad you decided to give in." Noah combed his fingers through the curls flowing over the pillow. "I don't make promises I can't keep, and I promise never to cheat on you with another woman. If you want something, all you have to do is ask, and I'll try and give it to you."

Her eyelids fluttered. "I don't want to talk about promises because I don't want to jinx what we have now."

Noah frowned. "I don't believe in jinxes or bad luck."

"What do you believe in, Noah?"

"That we're all responsible for our actions and that they have consequences."

"Sow the wind, reap the whirlwind," she said under her breath.

Noah nodded, his expression becoming serious. "Do

something wrong, and eventually you'll pay for it. It's the same with doing good."

"You're going to have to get off me," Viviana said, pushing against his shoulder. "You're too heavy."

He kissed her again. "That's because I probably outweigh you by at least a hundred pounds."

She rolled her eyes at him. "If you're trying to get me to tell you how much I weigh, then forget it. You should know never to ask a woman her age or her weight."

"That's something I learned a long time ago." He winked at her. "I'll be back as soon as I get rid of the condom."

Viviana lay back, watching Noah as he walked, naked and totally uninhibited, to the bathroom. She pulled the sheet up over her breasts and closed her eyes. She hadn't known how he would react to finding her in his bed, but she'd been willing to risk it.

There was something about Noah that had sparked a fire in her the first time he'd walked into her home. She'd felt as if he had special powers to look inside her to see what she'd vainly attempted to hide. He was the first man who'd stared at her and wordlessly communicated that he wanted her. Viviana was no stranger to men coming on to her with lame reasons why they wanted to take her out, and some were bold enough to say they wanted to sleep with her.

She believed she had been discriminating when it came to men, but that didn't change the fact her previous bad boyfriends took advantage of her specific blind spots and emotional vulnerabilities.

Noah was right about her having bad luck with the men she'd selected as boyfriends.

"What are you thinking about?"

She opened her eyes and smiled up at Noah looming over her. He had reentered the bedroom so quietly that she hadn't heard him. "I was thinking about the dog that stole my identity."

Noah flicked off the lamp, got into bed and pulled Viviana against his body. "Tell me about him."

"Didn't your investigator uncover information on him?"

"No, babe. I'd only asked him to investigate you. Do you want me to have him find the dog?"

"No, because sooner or later he's going to get caught. Once I realized he'd scammed me, I posted his photo on every available social-media site, which put women on notice not to fall for his lies." A beat passed. "Just say your investigator did find him, what would you do?"

"Hire someone to break his kneecaps."

She popped up, and Noah pulled her back down. "You wouldn't."

He chuckled softly "Of course not. What do you think your brother would've done if he'd caught up with him?"

"Lee would tease me saying if anyone messed me over, he'd snap their neck and then sit on their body until it got cold. Then he'd know they were gone for good."

"Well, damn!" Noah whispered. "I took one look at your brother and knew he wasn't to be played with."

"Lee isn't as dangerous as he appears. But he does have a way of looking at you that says *Don't get too close.*"

"The man's not dangerous, Viv. He's lethal."

"Why are you talking about my brother like that?" Viviana knew she sounded defensive, but for all of her life, with the exception of her aunt, there had only been her and Leland.

"I meant no harm, sweetheart. I don't have the skill to snap someone's neck, but I would stomp a mud hole in some dude's ass if he hurt my sister."

Viviana shifted, resting her leg over Noah's. "How did we just go from making love to talking about jacking people up?"

"Not *people*, Viv. Just your ex." Noah angled his head and covered her mouth in a surprisingly gentle kiss. "I want this to be the last time we talk about the folks in our past. Beginning tonight, it's only about us."

Parting her lips, Viviana, traced the outline of his mouth with the tip of her tongue. "Just us," she whispered, swallowing his breath as he exhaled. She kissed the pulsing hollow at the base of his throat, seemingly unable to get enough of tasting his warm skin. The scent from the bodywash he'd used to shower still lingered on his body. She let out a small shriek when Noah wrapped his arms around her waist and rolled her over and over on the king-size bed. She smiled up at him, her smooth legs sandwiched between his hairy ones.

Noah nuzzled her ear and then moved over to lie beside her. He could not stop asking himself how he had gotten so lucky to have fallen in love with someone like Viviana. She was a lot more complicated than any other woman he'd known, like a thousand-piece puzzle he had to complete to see the whole picture.

Jordan had asked when he was going to introduce her to their family, and he hadn't been able to give him a firm answer. However, he was confident that his parents would come to adore her as much as he did. He smiled when several wayward curls tickled his nose. He attempted to blow them off, but they floated back against his face.

"Are you falling asleep on me?"

Noah smiled. It was the same thing he'd asked Viviana what now seemed so long ago. "Nope. I'm just resting my eyes."

"So am I."

Why, he thought, did her voice sound so low and sexy with just a hint of a Southern drawl? The song "Take Me Home, Country Roads" popped into his head. Viviana had become his country mama, and the question was, if they were to have a future together, whether it would be easy for him to give up the bright lights of New York for a small town with two stoplights and a population of barely four thousand.

Although his cousin had made his home in Wickham Falls, there were times when Giles talked about missing the excitement of Manhattan and had finally been able to convince Mya to spend more than two months at a time in the city that never slept.

Mya had lived in Chicago when attending college, while Viviana had attended college in a small city in

North Carolina. Her entire life had revolved around small towns, and he wondered if she was afraid to live elsewhere. That was something he planned to discuss with her once their relationship reached the point where the issue would have to be resolved.

Viviana lay facedown on a deck chair as the sleek yacht sailed along the Intracoastal toward Fort Lauderdale. She did not want to believe the two weeks she had spent island-hopping with Noah were coming to an end. They'd spent their first week touring the entire resort, swimming in the ocean and in the infinity pool, picnicking on the beach and visiting the area where the farm animals were housed.

The island was divided into different areas: the above-water guesthouses for members of the Wainwright family and exclusive guests seeking ultimate privacy, and the section with tourists who'd reserved suites in two manor houses. At first she'd felt guilty, lazing around and doing absolutely nothing, but she soon became acclimated to what she deemed a somewhat self-indulgent lifestyle where all manner of food and drink were delivered by picking up a telephone and making the request.

As promised, she'd begun teaching Noah to cook, beginning with breakfast. He'd called the kitchen and asked for the foodstuff she needed, and he seemed genuinely interested when she demonstrated how to crack and whisk eggs, broil bacon to crispness, slice fruit and make fresh-squeezed orange juice. After three attempts, he was able to prepare a palatable breakfast and earn her seal of approval. Dinner proved to be more challenging, and Viviana decided let him bask in the knowledge that he'd done exceedingly well with only four lessons. Most evenings found them relaxing in the loggia at the rear of the house where the water appeared emerald green, giving the island its name.

Noah had broken up the monotony of lounging by suggesting they go island-hopping. He'd rented a yacht with a small crew, and every day they sailed to one or two islands to tour the ruins of sugar plantations or listen to griots. They would tell the history of the peoples brought over from foreign lands to work the plantations for European colonists, who grew wealthy from growing, processing and selling sugarcane. Viviana took pictures of crumbling remains of colonial mansions and sugar-processing plants, some nearly hidden by centuries of ivy, weeds and plants, and of fragrant flowers growing in wild abandon. She opened one eye and peered at Noah as he sat on a matching deck chair. He'd exchanged his shorts and tank top for a pair of slacks and a pullover sweater.

"The captain says he expects to dock within an hour."

Viviana nodded and sighed contentedly. Noah had chartered the boat for their return trip to the States in lieu of flying. "I need to go down below and change." Once they docked in Fort Lauderdale, she and Noah would board a charter to West Virginia before it continued on to New York City. She would have two days to recover from her Bahamian vacation ahead of leaving Wickham Falls to drive down to North Carolina to celebrate the Thanksgiving weekend with her family.

Viviana entered the cabin and closed the door. Fifteen minutes later she returned to the deck to stand at the rail with Noah to watch the skyline of Fort Lauderdale come into view. "I can't thank you enough for—"

Noah rested a hand over hers. "Stop, Viv. There's no need to thank me because I should be the one thanking you. You've made the past three weeks magical ones."

She gave him a sidelong glance. "Are you saying you'd want to do it again?"

"Yes. And the next time, I'd want more than three weeks."

"How much more time would you want?" she asked. "After all I do own a business."

"At least a couple of months."

"Where would you go?"

Noah wanted her to ask *Where would* we *go?* He didn't want to go away for any appreciable length of time without her but knew that would pose a problem once the B and B was back in business; it would only work if she trusted someone enough to manage it for her.

"Probably to South America and then on to Europe."

"You would fly there?"

"No. We'd charter a ship and stop and tour the countries we'd like to see."

Viviana took off her sunglasses and met his intense stare. "You can't make plans for us on a whim. Remember, I have a business to run, so it's not going to be easy for me to drop everything and go globe-trotting with you."

"What about Leland?"

"What about him?"

"Aren't you two partners?"

"Legally we are," Viviana confirmed. "Unofficially we aren't."

"Which is it, Viviana? Either you are or you aren't."

Noah struggled not to raise his voice or lose his temper. He realized his frustration stemmed from his inability to see her for the next two months. She had plans to celebrate Thanksgiving and Christmas with her family, while he would remain in New York until he received notice to return to Wickham Falls to attend the zoning hearing.

"Lee and I have joint ownership of the property, but he has relinquished all responsibility to me to operate the B and B. And he has two years before he completes the coursework for his degree in culinary arts. The last time I spoke to him, he said that Angela wants to stay in Charlotte to earn an undergraduate degree, which means they'll spend at least four years there before coming back to The Falls."

"You're going to spend the next four years running a business on your own?"

"Don't look at me like that, Noah," she spat out.

"Like what?" he returned.

"Like I don't have the wherewithal to do what I've been trained to do. I may not be the brightest bulb on the tree when it comes to picking boyfriends, but I'm not going to allow anyone to question whether I can run a business—with or without a partner."

Noah realized he'd just come down with the worst case of foot-in-mouth. He never should've questioned her ability to make the B and B a success. He rested a hand at the small of her back and felt her body go stiff. "I'm sorry, sweetheart. I'm not questioning your ability."

Viviana turned back to look at the choppy waters of the Intracoastal. "Remember, I have a staff that I'm paying with the money you gave me as a gap loan. Once the permits are approved and I reopen for the season, they will return to work, and we'll pick up from there."

He took a step, pressing his chest against her back and smiling when he felt her relax. Noah didn't want to fight with Viviana when they had so little time left together. He couldn't understand how he'd come to depend on her to fill up a part of his life he hadn't even been aware was missing. When he'd dated women in the past, it had been to fill the empty hours when he did not want to be alone. However, it was different with Viviana. She had become not only his friend and lover but also his confidante. He'd shared details of his father's infidelity with her that he had never spoken to anyone outside of his family. She was nonjudgmental, and he knew he could trust her with his family's secrets.

Noah loved her, and he had also fallen in love with her. Initially he'd believed he'd been drawn to her because of her stunning beauty. He had likened her to smoldering embers with an occasional flicker of bright light which told him she was cool, but if he touched her, then he would feel the heat from a passion she'd sought to hide from every man who'd come within a foot of her.

It hadn't been easy for him to scale the wall she had erected to keep men not only out of her bed but out of her life in general. Never had he worked so hard to get close to a woman, and that was how he'd realized she was worth the work and the wait.

"How long do you plan to stay in Charlotte?"

"I'm going to stay the weekend. Lee and Angela have to return to their classes on Monday. Lee is taking the family on a cruise for Christmas, and he invited Miss Joyce to join them. She's volunteered to chaperone Malcolm and Zoe so Lee and Angela can have a belated honeymoon. I did tease him about having a honeymoon on a ship with hundreds of screaming children, but he said he'll take whatever he can get."

"Anytime he and his wife want to get away for a while, I can always make arrangements for them to stay at Emerald Cove."

Viviana smiled. "I'll definitely let him know that."

"If you had to choose a place to honeymoon, where would you want to go?" Noah chided himself as soon as the query slipped past his lips. Why was he asking Viviana about honeymoons when he hadn't asked her to marry him? Was it wishful thinking?

"It would have to be Venice."

"Not Paris or Rome?"

She shook her head. "I've always fantasized about going to Venice during Carnival, where I'd wear a mask with my outrageously glamorous ball gown and hire a gondola to take me from palazzo to palazzo for the endless parties."

"You sound like a heroine in a romance novel."

"Haven't I been a romance-novel heroine these past three weeks?"

Noah pressed his mouth to her hair. "Yes, you have, and I've tried to live up to your image as your hero."

"You didn't have to try, Noah. You are my hero."

He wanted to tell her he wanted to continue being not only her hero but to also be her husband and the father of their children. "So, your plans are still on for celebrating Christmas in the desert?" he asked, deftly steering the topic away from them as a couple.

"Yes. It's probably going to feel strange seeing Christmas lights and decorations when it's eighty-five degrees."

Noah stared at the approaching shoreline as the sleek yacht left the Intracoastal and glided smoothly into one of the many canals lined by palm trees and high-end real estate. With hundreds of boats and canals, the port city was known as the Venice of America.

A member of the crew had brought their luggage on deck, and Noah knew what they had shared for the past three weeks was ending. That he probably wouldn't see Viviana again for another two months.

The captain deftly pulled the ship alongside a pier, and within minutes they were standing on a dock where a driver held up a placard with *Wainwright* printed in large black letters. Noah reached for Viviana's hand and led her over to where the man stood beside a town car.

"I'm Wainwright."

The ride to the Fort Lauderdale airport passed in a comfortable silence as he held Viviana's hand, and no words were exchanged between them during the flight to the Tri-State Airport because they weren't needed.

The small jet landed smoothly, and Viviana unbuckled her seat belt. "You don't have to get off with me," she said to Noah as he undid his belt.

"Baby…"

"Please, Noah. Don't make this harder for me than it is."

"This is not just about you."

Leaning forward, she placed her hand on his clean-shaven jaw. "Please. I'm begging you." Viviana prayed she wouldn't break down and start crying. She kissed him and then stood up and walked to the front of the aircraft and down the stairs to where a driver was loading her luggage into the trunk of a sedan. Within minutes of touching down, the flight crew had unloaded her bags.

She nodded to the driver when he opened the rear door for her. Tears blurred her vision as she attempted to buckle her seat belt. Viviana had fallen in love with Noah Wainwright, wanted to share her life with him, but feared that what she had shared with him in a tropical paradise was indeed a fantasy, and that now that she was back in the real world, it would vanish like a puff of smoke.

Chapter Ten

Viviana stared through the windshield and smiled when she saw her brother step out on to the porch of his late-model house in a new development in a Charlotte suburb. She'd left Wickham Falls at four in the morning to avoid the holiday traffic, and two hours later she entered the city limits for Charlotte, North Carolina.

Parking behind Angela's minivan, she shut off the engine and reached for her handbag and a tote filled with wrapped Christmas gifts on the passenger seat. Viviana noted that marriage agreed with her brother when he came over and opened her door. His lean face was fuller. He smiled.

Leland Remington stared at her as if she was a stranger. "Please don't tell me you've been going to a tanning salon."

Viviana laughed and went on tiptoe to kiss his cheek. "Bite your tongue, brother. When have you known me to need a tanning salon? I just got back from the Bahamas."

Leland took the bags from her loose grip. "How long were you there?"

"Three weeks."

"Who did you go with?"

She looped her arm through her brother's, and they climbed the porch together. "What makes you think I went with someone?"

Reaching over her head, Leland opened the door. "Because I happen to know my little sister better than she believes I do. You've never traveled alone."

She had to agree with Leland. He did know her well, perhaps better than she knew herself. They had always been open with each other, and she knew she'd disappointed him when she'd finally told him that she was going to lose the house. His voice had been very calm, almost emotionless, when he said he would take care of it. And his taking care of it translated into him filing discharge papers to become a civilian and return home in order to give her the financial support to save their ancestral home.

"I went with Noah Wainwright."

"Did you enjoy yourself?"

Viviana's jaw dropped. She hadn't expected him to ask her that. "Of course I did."

Leland stopped in the entryway and set the bags on a chair next to a table crowded with photographs of his and Angela's wedding and of Malcolm and Zoe at various ages. Light from the hallway fixture glinted off his wavy raven-black hair. Looking at him, Viviana realized her brother looked more and more like their father as he aged.

"I'm glad for you, Vivi. It's about time you met someone whose agenda is not to take advantage of you."

"When did you become a cheerleader for Noah?"

"When I sat down with the man to talk about selling off land we hadn't used and didn't need, I knew within a few minutes that he was someone I could trust. And if I could trust him, then I'd trust him with you. Anyone with eyes could see that the man was gaga over you—he couldn't stop staring. And even though you were giving the man attitude and the stink eye, he wasn't going to let that stop him from getting to you."

She flashed a demure smile. "Well, he did get to me when I finally agreed to become his date for a destination wedding. He extended the stay when we checked in to his family's vacation resort and went island-hopping. I bought gifts for you, Angela and the twins, but I don't want you to open them until Christmas."

Leland nodded. "I'll hide the bag in the crawl space."

Viviana glanced around the two-story house with an open floor plan. The entryway opened out to family, living and dining rooms that flowed into a state-of-the-art eat-in kitchen with a breakfast bar seating four. "How long do you plan to rent this house?"

"We decided to buy the house instead of renting it. I used my GI Bill."

She stared, shocked at this disclosure. "You're planning to live here permanently?"

"That's something I wanted to talk to you about in person."

"I'm here, Lee. So, please talk to me."

Viviana sat on a stool at the cooking island and listened intently as her brother told her that he and his wife had had a number of conversations about permanently relocating. Even though she hadn't wanted to leave Wickham Falls because her first husband and the father of her children was buried there, she wanted to start over without folks from The Falls pointing fingers and whispering about her marrying her late husband's best friend.

Suddenly she felt as if everyone she loved had moved away from Wickham Falls, leaving her totally alone to deal with some of the narrow-minded townspeople who refused to forget the atrocities perpetrated on their ancestors because of the Wolfes' need to control those who worked for them.

You should be happy for your brother because he has gone through enough with those who blamed him for the sins of our father, her silent voice taunted. "Angela's right, and you also need a new start, Lee. And based on what I saw on the way here, I think it's perfect for you and your family."

Leland gathered her close to his chest. "You're all right with me living here?"

"Of course I'm all right, Lee. In fact, I feel somewhat responsible for this new phase of your life."

"How's that, sis?"

"If I hadn't called to tell you I was drowning in debt and about to lose the house, you would've stayed in the army and probably wouldn't have had the chance to reunite with the girl who'd always had your heart."

His black sweeping eyebrows lifted. "You know about that?"

"Duh," she drawled. "I saw the way you used to look at Angela whenever she and Justin came to the house to study. You spent more time staring at her than you did at your books."

"Why didn't you say something?"

"Would you have believed me? You probably would've told me to mind my own business and that I was too young to know anything that went on between a boy and girl."

Leland nodded, smiling. "You're so right. Angela, Miss Joyce and the kids are still asleep. We were up late prepping everything, so the only thing we have to do is roast the turkey and put the sides in the oven. Miss Joyce is staying in the guestroom closest to the staircase, and Angela has prepared the other bedroom for you."

"Thanks, Lee. If it's all right with you, I'm going to get my bags and take a nap because I was up before the chickens to get down here, before the roads got too crowded."

"Go on upstairs. Your bedroom is the last one down the hall on the right. Give me your fob, and I'll bring your bags up and leave them outside the door."

Slipping off the stool, Viviana reached into her tote and handed Leland the fob to her car and then headed for the staircase. She was happy for her brother. He'd married the woman he'd always loved and was now father to two adorable children, lived in a modern sub-division and was studying to become a professional chef. He had finally gotten everything he'd wanted out of life, while her future was still in limbo.

Viviana was certain her application would be approved, and then she would be faced with waiting until it was reversed and she could reopen the B and B. She wasn't counting on locals to check in but tourists who occasionally came to the region to shop or tour some of the closed mines or those who were just passing through and needed a clean bed for the night.

"Good grief, girl, what happened to your face?"

Viviana smiled over Zoe's reddish hair at Joyce Mitchell as she walked into the kitchen. Angela's mother-in-law hadn't changed much. She had always been outspoken and said whatever came to her mind. "Hello, Miss Joyce. I was vacationing in the Bahamas."

Angela turned to look at her mother-in-law. "I think her tan is incredible. Her complexion is so even that she doesn't even need foundation."

Viviana gave her sister-in-law a barely perceptible wink. Her nap had been preempted when she heard someone tapping on the bedroom door. When she'd got up to answer, she saw Zoe looking up at her with a strange look on her little round face until she recognized Auntie Vivi. All sleep was forgotten when the three-year-old talked incessantly about her new house and how Viviana had to see her room because her dolls had their own house. Knowing she wasn't going back to sleep, she carried Zoe downstairs to the kitchen.

Angela was also up, and she ushered her children into the bathroom and instructed them to brush their teeth and take a bath before meeting company. Joyce was the last to get up, and she made a big show of kissing her grandchildren until they pushed her away.

"Did you go with a man?" the older woman asked.

"Yes, I did," Viviana said truthfully. She wasn't about to lie to the woman, because at twenty-nine, she felt she had to answer only to herself for her actions.

"Is it serious?" Joyce continued with her questioning.

Leland and Angela looked at Joyce as if she had taken leave of her senses for asking something so personal. "Nah," Viviana drawled nonchalantly. "We're just friends. He needed a date for his friend's wedding, and I agreed to be his plus-one." She knew if she didn't give Joyce an explanation, the woman would draw her own conclusions, and once back in The Falls, the rumors would spread like wildfire that the Wolfe girl was involved with a man. It didn't matter that she was a Remington, since to those in The Falls, she was and would always be a Wolfe.

Joyce pushed out her lips. "I wish someone would take me to the islands for a little rest and relaxation, too."

Leland turned to stare at her. "What do you think we were doing when Angela and I invited you to go with us on the cruise to the Caribbean?"

A flush suffused the older woman's light brown complexion. "I'm sorry. I forgot about that."

Zoe tugged on the end of Viviana's ponytail. "I like

your hair." The child's compliment shattered the tense silence.

Viviana kissed the red flyaway curls. "And I like your hair. I always wanted red hair because I have freckles. Somehow freckles and red hair go together."

The three-year-old touched her button nose. "I have spots on my nose."

"They're called freckles, sweetness," Viviana said.

Zoe laughed. "Daddy says I'm a sweet little girl."

Viviana stared over her head at Leland. "That's because your daddy is right."

Malcolm walked into the kitchen rubbing his eyes. "I'm still sleepy," he said around a wide yawn.

Angela took a carton of eggs out of the French-door refrigerator. "That's because someone doesn't want to go to bed when he's told."

Malcolm was the mirror image of his late father. He'd inherited his taupe-brown complexion, light brown eyes and curly hair. He patted Leland's arm to get his attention. "Daddy, can I go back to bed?"

Bending slightly, Leland scooped the boy up in his arms. "After you eat breakfast, you can go back to bed. Okay?"

Malcolm nodded. "Okay."

Viviana marveled at how easy it was for Leland to adapt to the role of father to Angela's twins. They had even talked to their grandmother about him legally adopting them, and Joyce Mitchell was in agreement when they informed her that her grandchildren would be known by Mitchell-Remington.

As soon as breakfast concluded, Leland took the

turkey out of the refrigerator to bring it to room temperature before he would put it into the oven. Viviana wanted to stay up and talk with Angela, but fatigue won over, and she retreated to her bedroom with Zoe in tow, and they climbed into bed together and fell asleep.

Viviana waited until Monday to drive back to Wickham Falls. She'd spent four fun-filled days with her family. Leland did all of the cooking, and after dinner everyone would retreat to the lower level that had been converted into space for relaxing and entertaining. She watched animated movies with her niece and nephew and joined Leland when he turned on the large wall-mounted television to watch college and professional football games.

She discovered that interacting with Malcolm and Zoe stirred latent maternal instincts for the first time in her life. She played house with Zoe, and they sat on the floor pretending they were having a tea party. Viviana didn't begrudge her brother his happiness, but it did remind her of how lonely her life had become. All of her college girlfriends lived in other states, and she had lost contact with the girls with whom she had gone to the parochial school.

She thought she wouldn't have felt so isolated if the B and B was open for business. Even if she only had one guest, she would feel better knowing someone other than herself was in the house.

Viviana found herself checking her cell phone to see if she'd missed a call or text from Noah, but she'd gotten only two texts since leaving him on the plane at the Tri-State Airport. She was beginning to think he was the type of man who subscribed to a philosophy of out of sight, out of mind. She lost track of the number of times she'd picked up her phone to call him, but the voice in her head said she was a fool to chase a man who didn't think enough of her to call and want to talk to her.

By midweek, the urge to call him proved too much, and she tapped his number. It rang three times before she heard a woman's voice. "Hello."

Viviana hesitated over hanging up. "I'm sorry, but I must have dialed the wrong number."

"Is this Viviana Remington?"

She went completely still. "Yes, it is. Who's asking?"

"I'm Chanel, Noah's sister. When he came back from vacation, he complained about not feeling well but couldn't stop talking about you. Right now, Noah is sick with the flu. In fact, everyone in the house has it. I'm the only one who isn't sick, so I'm keeping my fingers crossed it will pass me by."

Viviana felt her stomach knot up. "How is he?"

"Not good. We had to call the doctor because he's been throwing up. I tried to get him to drink some water, but he can't keep anything down. I'm afraid he's going to become dehydrated, and he'll have to be hospitalized and given fluids intravenously."

"I'm coming up to New York."

"Stay the hell where you are because you don't want what we have here. We even banned Giles from the house because we don't want him to give it to Mya."

Chanel mentioning Giles's wife reminded Viviana

that Mya was in the early stages of her pregnancy. "You have my number, so I want you to call me and give me updates on his condition. And tell him if he doesn't try to take some liquids, I am coming up to New York to wait until he's feeling better, then I'm going to break up with him. Make certain you tell him exactly what I've just said."

There came a beat. "I will, Viviana." There was another pause. "Are you in love with my brother?"

"Yes, I am." What did his sister expect her to do? Lie?

"Good, because it's obvious he's crazy about you."

"Don't forget to call me, Chanel."

"I won't. Viviana?"

"Yes?"

"When will the family get to meet you?"

Viviana noticed she'd said *the family* as if the entire Wainwright clan had to give their seal of approval for her to be accepted to date Noah. "I don't know, Chanel. Maybe we'll get to meet each other sometime next year."

"I can't wait. I'll tell Noah you called."

"Thank you."

Viviana ended the call and chided herself for harboring negative thoughts. The man she loved hadn't been able to call her because he was sick, and she was ready to kick him to the curb. And Chanel mentioning Mya's condition reminded her to buy fabric to make a crib quilt or two. She'd promised Seth that she would make one for his wife once they announced they were having a baby; meanwhile, she had nothing but time to make a few for Mya.

* * *

Chanel sent her daily texts, with accompanying emojis, on Noah's condition and attitude. They went from angry faces to one with a mouth covered with a band of expletives. She said that he had lost his voice but he'd said as soon he was able to talk, he would call her. Thankfully he was on a light diet and beginning to take liquids. Everyone was recovering, albeit slowly, and were in better spirits now and getting into the mood of the holiday, now that the staff had begun putting up Christmas decorations.

Viviana kept busy putting together squares of fabric by hand. Her aunt had taught her to quilt by hand because she claimed it was more authentic than using a sewing machine. It was more laborious and she was careful to make certain all of her stitches were the same. When she'd walked into the department store in town, she went directly to the section where she could find the needlecraft supplies and spent more than hour going through fat quarters, thread, needles and thimbles. She'd also bought knitting needles, crochet hooks and baby yarn in soft pastel shades. She knew she was buying duplicates because her aunt had packed away all of her needlecraft supplies in the attic, but Viviana did not want to lift and shift cartons until she found what she needed.

Placing a cloth over the table in the kitchen, she placed the backing for one quilt over the cloth and then strategically pinned the squares. To save time, Viviana decided to attach the squares to the backing with yarn and secure each corner with a neatly tied bow.

She'd just finished threading a yarn needle when her cell phone rang.

A slight frown furrowed her forehead when she recognized her aunt's number. "Hello, Aunt Babs."

"Hey, baby. How are you?"

"I'm good. How's my uncle?"

"He's also good. I'm calling to tell you we're not going to be here for Christmas. We entered a contest hosted by our church's fund-raiser and won first prize. We're going to Rome for Midnight Mass at St. Peter's. I'm sorry to call you so late because I know you've bought your ticket, so let me know what you paid for it, and I'll reimburse you."

Viviana collapsed on the chair like a ragdoll. First her brother was going out of the country, and now her aunt and uncle. "Don't worry about the money, Aunt Babs. The ticket is refundable. I can always use the money for another trip."

"That makes me feel a little better. But I'm still sorry—"

"Please don't apologize. You've been talking about going to Rome for Christmas for as long as I can remember, and now it's going to happen."

"I promise to bring back something nice for you."

"You don't have to do that. Just be safe."

"Thank you, Vivi. I love you, baby."

Viviana smiled. "I love you, too."

She ended the call, closed her eyes and gritted her teeth. It wouldn't be the first Christmas she would be alone, but it was the first time that she wanted to spend it with someone she truly loved. Well, she was a big girl, and as such, she had to adjust to the unexpected. Viviana opened her eyes and went back to finishing the quilt. It had taken her five days to complete one crib quilt, and instead of beginning another, she had decided to crochet a pair of baby booties.

Her head had barely touched the pillow when the cell phone vibrated on the bedside table. Reaching for it, Viviana peered at the screen. Noah was calling her. "How are you feeling?"

"A lot better than I was a few days ago."

"You sound hoarse."

"Today is the first day I can speak above a whisper."

She sat up and adjusted the pillows behind her back. "Does it hurt to talk?"

"No. That's what's so funny. One day the voice just went, and I couldn't even squeak. Chanel told me what you said about breaking up with me. Did you mean it?"

"Of course I meant it. I didn't fall in love with you to have you die on me because you were too pigheaded to take something to help you get better."

"I forgot that you told me you loved me."

"Did you also have a bout of amnesia along with the flu?"

"I don't think so. What have you been doing down there in The Falls?"

"Making crib quilts and baby clothes."

"You're pregnant!"

"Stop it, Noah Wainwright. You know right well I'm not pregnant."

"How would I know? We haven't seen each other in weeks."

"You're right."

"Why are you making baby things?"

"Now that I have nothing but time on my hands, I decided to get a jump on making a few things for Mya's baby."

"What are you talking about, Viv?"

Viviana told him about her aunt's call and the change of plans about celebrating Christmas in Arizona.

"Are you saying you're going to spend Christmas alone?" Noah asked.

"Yes, and it wouldn't be the first time I've been alone on Christmas." She didn't tell him she'd discovered Marcus's subterfuge and given him his walking papers a week before Christmas.

"Not this year, Viviana Remington. You're coming up to New York."

"Are you asking or ordering me, Noah?"

"I'm sorry about that," he apologized. "I'd like to invite you to spend Christmas and New Year's with my family here in New York."

"I really don't want to intrude—"

"Don't even go there," he said threateningly. "How the hell would you be an intrusion when I've told everyone about you?"

"You shouldn't have done that."

"What? Not tell my family that I've found a woman who completes me? Give me a few days to make arrangements to fly you up here."

"That's not necessary. I can change my ticket from Arizona to New York."

"Is that what you want?"

"Yes." Did he really believe she was too good to fly with regular people?

"Text me once you confirm your flight, and I'll arrange for ground transportation. Don't forget to pack winter clothes because it's been very cold up here."

"Okay," she said.

"The Wainwrights always host a formal New Year's Eve fund-raiser, so if you don't have something to wear, I'll ask my sister to take you shopping."

"Thanks for the offer, but I'm certain I can find something in my closet," she lied smoothly. She didn't have anything for a formal affair, and that meant she had to go shopping for a dress and accessories. "Hang up, and save your voice."

"Okay. I love you to death, Viviana Remington."

Viviana smiled. "That goes double for me, Noah Wainwright." Tapping the screen, she ended the call and fell back against the pillows. "I'm going to spend Christmas with the man I love," she said aloud. She'd wait until the morning to call the airline and change her ticket.

Chapter Eleven

Viviana spied Noah holding a sign with her name. He was dressed entirely in black: jacket, pullover sweater, slacks and shoes. When he'd said he would arrange ground transportation, she hadn't thought he would accompany her into Manhattan himself. And it was obviously he'd lost weight because his face was a lot leaner. However his tan hadn't completely faded.

"I'm Ms. Remington."

He smiled and brushed a light kiss over her mouth. "Welcome to New York." He took the garment bag containing her dress from her. "How many bags do you have?"

"One Pullman."

"As soon as it comes off the conveyor, we'll be on our way."

"Wait here," she told him. "I'll get it."

Viviana had admitted to Noah that she loved him, but only after seeing him again had she realized the depth of her feelings for him. She'd told herself over and over that she wasn't attracted to nor would she date a man that looked like Noah, and in the end she had wasted time and lost money on men who were the complete opposite of him in every way. And if someone had accused her of being biased or bigoted, she would've openly denied it.

However, she felt she was luckier than a lot of women who'd searched all of their lives and never found their romance-novel heroes. Perhaps, she mused, she'd had to kiss a few frogs in order to find her prince. She watched for her bag, and when she saw it, she edged her way closer to the conveyer to snag it. Noah had come over to take it from her.

"I'm parked outside."

The instant the terminal doors opened, Viviana felt the frigid air hit her face, and she sucked in her breath. She followed Noah to a black Mercedes Benz parked at the curb. The trunk opened smoothly, and the driver got out and came around to open the rear door. She slipped onto the leather seat, unaware that she was shivering. Noah had said it was cold but not freezing.

Noah got in beside her and pulled her close. "Did you bring gloves?"

"No. I didn't think it would be this cold."

"We had a trace of snow on Thanksgiving, and ever since then the temperatures have been hovering around freezing."

She rested her head on his shoulder. "How are you feeling?"

"I'm good."

"You've lost weight."

"I haven't weighed myself, but I'm certain I'll gain it back during the week."

Viviana looked up at him. His hair was longer, the ends touching the tops of his ears. He was back to looking like a surfer. "Have the people in your family recovered?"

"Everyone's getting there. This Christmas is going to be a lot quieter than usual. But we'll still get together on Christmas for a buffet dinner and open presents around midnight before we bed down for the night."

"Is there enough room in your house for everyone to claim a bed?"

Noah smiled. "Are you asking if we'll be sharing a bedroom?" She nodded. "No, we won't. My parents are old-fashioned about unmarried couples sleeping together. My brothers and I weren't permitted to bring girls home and have them spend the night. It's the reason my brother Rhett is moving out. When my mother discovered a girl in his bed, she went ballistic. I felt sorry for the girl, but it wasn't her fault. Rhett knows the rules."

"What did you do when you wanted to have sex with someone?"

"I paid to check in to a hotel. That is, if she didn't have her own place."

"I suppose if you're grown enough to have sex, then

you should be grown enough to take it where you can have complete privacy," Viviana said.

"Now you sound like Christiane. My mother can be a little snobbish, but she's right about laying down the law with her sons, because she didn't want them to use her home as a motel for what she called *licentious behavior*." Noah kissed Viviana's hair. "I wanted to use this week to take you to the Rockefeller Center to see the tree and maybe even go ice-skating, but the doctor warned me to stay away from crowds."

"I don't need you to take me around, Noah. Just being in New York with you is enough."

He met her eyes. "Is it?"

Viviana smiled. "Of course it is. It's going to be nice seeing Mya and Lily again."

"I'm going to tell you now that my parents can't wait to meet you."

"What have you told them about me?"

"That you're smart, creative and very beautiful."

She patted his chest over his sweater. "You sound biased."

"Damn right."

Viviana shifted to stare out the side window as they exited the airport and headed for Manhattan. She'd come to New York a few times, but it was always to visit friends who lived in the suburbs with one- and two-family homes and with several cars lining the driveways. Only once had she ventured into Manhattan and found herself overwhelmed by the number of people jostling for space along crowded sidewalks and by the flow of traffic where pedestrians played a game of chicken with aggressive cab drivers.

"Do you like living here?" she asked Noah.

"Yes. It's all I know."

"Would you ever consider living anywhere else?"

"It would all depend on the circumstances. Why do you ask, Viv?"

"I just..." Her words trailed off just as her cell phone rang. She picked up her cross-body bag and took out the phone. *Wickham Falls Town Hall* appeared on the screen. "Hello?"

"Viviana Remington?" asked a strong male voice.

"This is she."

"Ms. Remington, I really shouldn't be calling to tell you this and I could get fired if someone finds out, but I'm certain you'd want to know the status of your application to reverse your property from commercial to personal."

"Of course I do." She hadn't expected to hear from anyone until January.

"I'm sorry to tell you that your application was denied."

She felt as if someone had punched her in the stomach. "Why?"

"The vote was three for and four against."

Viviana stared at Noah staring back at her. "This may sound a little unethical, but could you please tell me who voted it down?"

There was a pregnant pause before he said, "I'm only going to tell you because I enlisted in the army with your brother and he had always been a straight-up guy.

If you tell anyone I told you, I'll deny it. It was our newest member, Myles Duncan who'd cast the deciding no vote. Again, I'm sorry."

"So am I. Thank you so much. And I promise not to tell anyone what you've just told me."

"Once you get your written notice, you can come in and appeal it."

She nodded, her head moving up and down like a bobblehead doll. "Thank you, and I hope you have a very Merry Christmas."

"I'm wishing you the same."

"What was that all about?" Noah watched Viviana as she dropped the phone in her lap.

He had only heard one side of her conversation, but her body language indicated that whoever had called her had given her bad news.

"That was someone from the town hall who said my application was denied."

"Why?"

"He didn't say, but I have a good reason to know why."

"What are you talking about?"

She closed her eyes and leaned her head against the headrest. "Whenever there's a vote on an issue, it needs a majority to pass. The zoning board has seven members, and the newest member was the dissenting vote.

Myles Duncan is nothing more than a vindictive jerk. He once asked me out when we both were in high school, and I turned him down because I had no interest in him."

Noah forced a smile he didn't quite feel. "High school boys can be jerks," he said in agreement.

"What are we going to do about the rejection?"

Wrapping his arms around her body, Noah rested his chin on the top of Viviana's head. "Don't worry, sweetheart. We'll figure out something."

"I was told we can appeal."

"Before we do that, I'll talk to my father. When it comes to real estate law and loopholes, I'm certain he'll be able to find something we can use once you appeal."

"I hope you're right."

Noah smiled in spite of the situation. "The Wainwrights eat, sleep and breathe real estate, Viv. And we have enough lawyers on staff to find some arcane law to reverse the decision. I don't want you to worry your beautiful head about this because it is a time for celebrating and not crying. Haven't you heard *There's no crying in real estate*?"

She glanced up at him. "I thought it was *There's no crying in baseball.*"

"That, too," he said with a wide grin.

Viviana knew her mouth was gaping when the driver pulled up in front a four-story greystone building facing Central Park and spanning a half block of Fifth Avenue. Massive oak doors adorned with large pine wreaths and velvet bows opened, and an elderly, formally dressed butler waited as they alighted from the sedan.

He nodded to Noah. "Good evening, Master Noah."

Noah smiled. "Good evening, Walter." He took off his jacket and handed it to the man.

The man Noah called *Walter* stared at her, and then she realized he was waiting for her coat. She unbuttoned it, and Noah slipped it off her shoulders and handed it to the butler. "Thank you."

Walter nodded again. "Welcome, Ms. Remington." He shifted his attention to Noah. "Madam Wainwright has held off serving dinner until you arrived. She's in the small dining room."

Viviana's eyebrows lifted slightly. It was apparent he'd known she was coming. She followed Noah into the expansive entrance hall with priceless Persian and Aubusson rugs scattered about gleaming marble floors. The mansion was decorated for the season, but Noah was walking so fast she didn't have time to see everything. She was practically running to keep up with his longer legs.

She saw his mother standing behind a chair with a table set for four. There were water goblets and wine glasses at each place setting. When Walter had mentioned the small dining room, Viviana could not have imagined a room which could comfortably hold more than a dozen, with more than enough space for ample movement, as small. She felt wholly underdressed in a pair of jeans, pullover cotton T-shirt and low-heeled booties when she saw Christiane's powder blue raw-silk blouse, navy gabardine-wool pencil skirt and matching Ferragamo pumps.

The older woman's emerald green eyes shimmered like polished gems. Her straight platinum hair was cut into a becoming bob. She extended her hands. "It's so nice to finally meet you. I must say you're truly lovely."

Viviana took the proffered hands and pressed her cheek to Christiane's cool one. "Thank you for opening your home to me for the holidays." The distinctive scent of Chanel No. 5 wafted to her nostrils.

Christiane sniffed the air. "Are you wearing Shalimar?"

Viviana smiled. It was apparent Christiane was more than familiar with classic perfumes. "Yes. My mother used to wear it. I always thought it was too mature for me until I turned twenty-five, and I've been wearing it ever since."

Christiane leaned closer. "I usually judge the women my sons date by the perfume they wear. If they have on No. 5, Joy, L'Air du Temps, Shalimar or Miss Dior and not some drugstore brand, I know they like to pamper themselves with only the best."

Viviana recalled Noah saying this woman was a snob, and it was apparent the choice of one's perfume was important as to whether she would accept or reject her son's choice in a woman. Jeans notwithstanding, it was apparent she had passed the test.

"I have a weakness for perfume," Viviana admitted.

Christiane smiled. "Now I know we're really going to get along." She looked at Noah over Viviana's head. "Noah, darling, please show your girlfriend where she can wash up."

"Where's Dad?" he asked Christiane.

"He's in his study returning a phone call. If he's not finished by time you come back, then we'll start without him. Since there are only the four of us, I decided we would dine buffet-style." She looked at Viviana. "I don't know if you eat red meat, but let me warn you that we Wainwrights are carnivores. I did have the chef prepare a few vegetarian plates like couscous, quinoa and tabbouleh."

"I eat everything," Viviana said, hoping to reassure Christiane that she wasn't a picky eater.

"Good for you. Now, go and wash up because I know the only thing those folks gave you during your flight was pretzels or cookies. You'd think they'd offer you more than a bunch of salty or sweet snacks after what they charge."

Noah took Viviana's hand, lacing their fingers together. "Shame on you, Mother. When was the last time you took a commercial carrier to know what they serve?"

Christiane waved her hand. "Go and wash up because I'm certain your girlfriend is starving."

Noah steered Viviana out of the dining room and down a narrow hallway to a bathroom. "You'll have to forgive my mother."

Turning on the faucet in one of the twin marble sinks, Viviana stared him in the mirror. "Forgive her for what? I think she's charming."

"You don't think she's a snob?"

"Don't, Noah. Your mother is who she is, and I wouldn't want her to change and become something she's not, just to make me feel comfortable. I am who I am, and what you see is what you get."

Noah winked at her. "And I happen to like what I see." He dried his hands on a towel before handing her one. "I hope you won't mind sharing a suite with my sister. Right now, she's hanging out with Giles's sister Skye, who just broke up with her bum-ass fiancé and moved back home."

"Where did she live before?"

"Seattle. I think he encouraged her to move there so he could control her and her money. Even though Skye had come into her trust, she wasn't so in love that she'd let some man pimp her." Noah let out a groan when he saw Viviana's pained reflection in the mirror. "I'm sorry, babe. That was thoughtless of me to say that."

Viviana dried her hands and wrapped her arms around his waist. "There's no need to apologize, darling. I'm over it."

He wanted to tell Viviana she wasn't over it. At least, not yet. Not until she trusted him enough to know that he would never take advantage of her, that he wasn't like the other men in her past. "Come on, let's go back before my mother reads me the riot act."

"Something smells good," she said as they walked toward the dining room.

"Our chef is one of the best in the city," Noah announced proudly. "We found him when we had a catered affair at a hotel, and my father made him an offer he couldn't refuse. He doubled his salary and offered him his own suite of rooms on the lower level."

"How many rooms are in this house?"

"I think there may be between eighteen and twenty. If you want to know for certain, then you'll have to ask my mother." Noah rested his hand at the small of Viviana's back as he escorted her into the dining room.

Edward flashed a warm smile as they walked in. "Well, it's about time." He came over to hug Viviana and kiss her cheek. "We've been waiting to meet you ever since my son started talking nonstop about you."

Viviana met a pair of laughing light blue eyes. "You can't believe everything he says because there are times when he tends to embellish a few things," she said, offering him a friendly smile. She felt as if she'd been put on the spot and wondered exactly what Noah had told his family about her.

Edward patted her cheek. "This time he told the truth. You are lovely." He picked up a plate from a stack on the buffet server and handed her one. "Come eat."

The chef had prepared dishes featuring a Mediterranean theme: grilled lamb rib chops, lamb meatballs with tzatziki, hummus, spinach pie, couscous and tabbouleh, stuffed grape leaves, and grilled pork souvlaki.

"Everything looks delicious."

"That's because it is," Christiane confirmed. "I always take a little of each, then go back for seconds."

Viviana decided to take Christiane's lead and take small servings from each server. Noah pulled out a chair at the table and seated her. She waited until everyone had served themselves and sat down.

Noah filled her water goblet from a fully leaded carafe, then Christiane's, his own, and then handed the carafe to Edward. "Would anyone like wine?"

"I'll take merlot," Edward said.

Christiane smiled at her son. "I'll also have merlot."

Viviana saw three pairs of eyes trained on her. "I'll pass."

"Are you in the family way?"

"Mom!"

"Christiane!"

Noah and Edward had spoken in unison.

Viviana shook her head. "No, I'm not."

"Are you sure?" Christiane questioned.

"I'm one hundred percent sure." She remembered Noah telling her about his mother's craving for another grandchild. Whenever she and Noah made love, there was never a time when he did not protect her, and she'd made an appointment to see her gynecologist to ensure she would not conceive at this time in her life.

Viviana had to agree with Noah as to the chef's proficiency creating dishes with flavors that tantalized her palate as she listened intently to Christiane talk about the changes she wanted to make to their upcoming annual fund-raising event. "How many do you expect to attend?" she asked.

Christiane peered at her over the rim of her water goblet. "We limit it to one hundred."

"Is it sit-down or buffet?"

"It has always been a buffet. Why do you ask?"

Viviana had put on her hospitality/banquet manager–hat when she listened to Christiane talk about the New Year's Eve fund-raiser. "How difficult would it be for you and your staff to have a sit-down dinner?"

Christiane blinked slowly. "It wouldn't be that difficult if I hired additional staff to serve."

"What are you thinking about?" Edward asked.

Viviana told them about working at the hotel where clients booked parties, some that included up to hundreds of guests. They would begin with a cocktail hour with hors d'oeuvres and carving stations, followed by a sit-down dinner. "I noticed the grand hall when I came in, and it could easily accommodate one hundred for the cocktail hour."

"You're right," Edward confirmed. "We have two ballrooms, and everyone usually gathers in the larger one."

"I really don't intend to meddle in something which has worked for you for so many years, but I always feel a sit-down dinner is more intimate, and it can bring strangers together. Rather than have ten tables with ten guests at each table, why don't you set up two banquet tables seating fifty at each and a head table for the hosts? Separate couples and intersperse family members among the guests."

Christiane pressed her palms together. "If they can feed one hundred at a state dinner in Buckingham Palace, then there's no reason why we can't do it here. And it has to be less chaotic with a sit-down affair. Viviana, I know you didn't come here to work, but I would truly appreciate your assistance in pulling this off. I sent out invitations for one hundred and so far have received responses from sixty that they are coming. If we end up with seventy-five to eighty, then I would consider that a wonderful return. Those who decline always donate to the earmarked charity, which makes the fund-raiser very successful. And whatever we raise, the Wainwright Foundation will match dollar for dollar."

Viviana thought how different the Wainwrights were from the Wolfes. They opened their home every year to host a gathering for a charitable cause, while the Wolfes only entertained politicians whom they could call on, if need be, to support their unscrupulous business practices.

"I'd love to help out anyway I can."

"You may come to regret saying that," Edward said under his breath. "My wife can be a beast when it comes to her social causes."

Viviana smiled at him and then covered her mouth with her hand in an attempt to smother a yawn. "I don't mind working hard if it is for a good cause." She ignored Noah when he nudged her foot with his under the table. She hadn't come to New York to be waited on hand and foot but to get to know his family.

She'd only just met Noah's mother and father but found them to be utterly unpretentious, despite the fact Noah claimed his mother was a snob. Perhaps she had been earlier in her life, but as a middle-aged grandmother, she struck Viviana as humble and down-to-earth.

Christiane folded her napkin and placed it next to her plate. "Noah, Viviana must be exhausted from traveling, so could you please show her to Chanel's room? Chanel called right after you left to go to the airport to say she's spending the night at Pat and Amanda's. Skye needs her support because she's still devastated about breaking up with her fiancé."

Pushing back his chair, Noah stood. "She should be celebrating instead of crying because if she'd married that clown, she would've gotten herself into something that—"

"Don't, Noah," Christiane warned softly, cutting him off. "You know we don't get into other folks' business when it comes to whom they choose to marry, because it always boomerangs when they turn on you."

"Your mother's right," Edward said. "It's apparent my niece had had enough of her fiancé's attempt to control her life and decided to end it. She's going to shed a few tears, but later on down the road she'll realize she made the right decision."

Noah pulled back Viviana's chair and assisted her to stand. "He's lucky Giles didn't go out to Seattle and kick his ass."

Christiane's face turned beet red. "Noah! You know I don't abide cursing in my home."

He put his arm around Viviana's waist. "You'll have to talk to Grandpa about that. He's the one who taught us how to curse."

Edward glared at his son. "Just because my father likes to occasionally remind people that he grew up cursing because he was a street kid, I don't want my children mimicking that type of behavior."

"I'm sorry, Mother, Dad."

Viviana waited until they were out of earshot to confront Noah. "You weren't sorry, and you know it."

He smiled down at her. "They know that. You'll probably get to meet my grandfather tomorrow. He's still recovering from the flu, and at eightysomething, he has to be very careful it doesn't turn into pneumonia. Dad hired a private-duty nurse to monitor him, and I'm willing to bet he's cursing the poor woman from A to Z."

"Did he really grow up on the streets?" Viviana asked as Noah punched the button for an elevator built into an alcove. The doors opened, and they walked into the car lined with mirrors. He punched a button for the third floor.

"Grandpa is what folks call an OG. An *original gangster*. He built WDG from scratch with nothing more than a few thousand dollars and nerves of steel. One of these days, I'll tell you all about the miscreants in my family, so don't think the Wolfes have a monopoly on immoral behavior."

The doors opened, and Viviana found herself in a carpeted hallway with silk-covered walls. "How many suites are on this floor?"

"Two. My parents and Chanel are on this floor. Jordan, Rhett and I had suites on the second floor, while the three on the top floor are set aside for houseguests. My mother decided to have you share Chanel's room because, come Christmas Eve, the rest of the family will join us and stay overnight, and this place will look like a frat house with people coming and going."

"Who lives on the first floor?"

"Grandpa. Once he started complaining about arthritis in his knees, he moved to the first floor."

"But you have an elevator," Viviana said.

"Grandpa doesn't like elevators because he was stuck in one during a blackout, and ever since then, he's been reluctant to get into one by himself. When he used to go into the office, he'd wait until someone rode up with him."

Viviana knew it would take time for her to come to know the quirks and idiosyncrasies of the people in Noah's large, extended family. And that was something she wouldn't be able to accomplish in a week.

Noah opened a door, and she walked into what she thought of as an apartment. It contained an en suite bath, dressing room, living/dining room and a utility kitchen. She found her luggage on a rack in the enormous bedroom with both a queen and a full-size bed. Her garment bag lay over the smaller bed.

Viviana walked over to the floor-to-ceiling windows and peered through the silk drapes. The suite overlooked Central Park. She could detect lightly falling snow under the glow of street lights. Turning around, she smiled at Noah. "I'm going to enjoy sleeping here."

He nodded. "If you need me for anything, just send me a text, and I'll be up."

"Oh no. I'll not have your mother giving me the stink eye if she catches you in my room."

"I'd never put you in a compromising position where you'd have to defend yourself." He smiled. "Good night, sweetheart."

"Good night, Noah."

He was there, then he was gone, closing the door behind him. Viviana suspected he still wasn't feeling well and was putting on a good face. She'd noticed that he'd picked at the food on his plate and preferred drinking water to wine. She'd come to New York to see her man, celebrate the holidays with his family and, hopefully, sort out her feelings for the man with whom she had fallen in love. She loved him, but she wasn't ready to plan a future with him.

Chapter Twelve

It was another two days before Noah was able to get his father alone to give him an update on the stalled Wickham Falls project. Edward was dividing his time between going into the office and working from home.

Noah sat on a butter-soft leather chair in Edward's study and propped his feet on a matching footstool. He told his father everything from filing the application to Viviana's telephone call from someone on the board. At first he'd thought Edward wasn't listening because he had his eyes closed, but when he'd opened them, they weren't the constantly laughing ones that met people even in serious circumstances.

Reaching for a pen in a desk filled with stacks of paper, Edward jotted down some notes. "You say they needed a majority, but there was one holdout."

Noah nodded. "Viviana said his name is Myles Duncan. I don't know if it's *Myles* with a *y* or an *i*."

"It doesn't matter. Why would he reject the application?"

"Viviana believes he was being vindictive because as a girl she refused to date him."

"What the hell!" Edward shouted. "He gets turned down by a girl, and years later he can't let it go?"

"Apparently that's what it is."

Edward shook his head. "If I had a dollar for every girl that refused to go out with me, I would've been sitting pretty before I turned eighteen."

"Well, the problem was this creep was still in high school. When I finally got Viviana to open up about it she said he was a senior and she was still a freshman."

Slumping back in the executive chair, Edward crossed his arms over his chest. "So, the predator was hunting young, innocent girls."

"That's what it sounds like."

Edward sat straight. "I'm going to call Pat and ask him to put one of his men on this. There has to be some obscure law on the books in West Virginia where you might be able to get it reversed without filing an appeal."

"Thanks, Dad. I really appreciate it."

"There's no need to thank me. After all, WDG has a stake in this. There's always more than one way to skin a cat." He peered closely at Noah. "You still look a little green around the gills. Why don't you go upstairs and get some rest before the gang descends on us tonight? Your mother and your girlfriend are now thick as thieves, so you don't have to concern yourself with entertaining her."

Noah knew his father was right. He still wasn't feeling one hundred percent, and he only got to see Viviana whenever they sat down to eat. His mother had the chauffeur on speed dial to drive her and Viviana around the city, picking up last-minute gifts for the staff, friends and family.

"I'm going to take your advice and turn in."

"Thanks for not challenging me, son."

"It's been a while since I challenged you, Dad."

Edward's pale eyebrows inched up his forehead. "Oh really? I remember a few months ago when you threatened to use your own money for the West Virginia project if I didn't approve the expenditure. And I only did that because I knew I would've lost you like I did Jordan."

"Lost me how?"

"Jordan has vowed never to work for WDG because of what your grandfather and I did to his and your biological mother. It was unconscionable, but at twenty-two I was too cowardly to stand up to my father. I was in love with Jordan's mother while engaged to your mother. And I would've married his mother, if your grandfather hadn't threatened to cut me off without a penny. But you and Rhett are different. You've always stood up for yourselves and are not afraid to fight for what you're passionate about."

Noah lowered his feet and stood. "I'd appreciate any help you can give." He'd thanked his father, when he wanted to tell him that he was facing the greatest challenge of his life thus far. He was in love with a woman he wanted to marry yet knew if he proposed, she would turn him down. He'd told himself over and over to be patient, yet he couldn't rid himself of the nagging feeling that if he waited too long, he would lose Viviana—not to another man but to another factor that would take precedence. Once her B and B was operational, he knew it would be all-consuming for her, leaving little room in her life for romance.

Viviana sat on the floor in the entrance hall cradling a sleeping Lily Wainwright on her lap. She hadn't known what to expect when attending her first Wainwright Christmas Eve celebration, but it had begun with an ongoing brunch for arriving family members. Everyone bedded down in the early afternoon to rest before the nighttime festivities.

The banquet table in the larger ballroom groaned with food as four generations of Wainwrights sat down to eat, drink, talk and laugh in abandon. Everyone was casually dressed, and once dinner concluded, they filed out of the ballroom and into the hall to sing Christmas carols and open gifts. The eight-foot Norway spruce covered with hundreds of priceless fragile glass ornaments going back several centuries was the focal point in the space with a twenty-foot ceiling.

She stared at Wyatt Wainwright, the family patriarch sitting on a rocker with a cashmere throw covering his legs, staring back at her. She'd met the octogenarian earlier that morning, and despite his advancing years, his laser-blue eyes were clear and alert. And when she saw him and Jordan together, the resemblance between the older man and his first grandson was obvious. Many of the younger children were sprawled out, sleeping on the priceless rugs, but their parents were loath to move them until all of the gifts had been opened.

Viviana held her breath when Edward held up one of her gifts and handed it to Mya. There was chorus of approval when Mya held up the handmade crib quilt and a pair of mint-green booties with a matching hat. She smiled when Mya blew her a kiss.

Edward picked up another one of her gifts, handing it to Noah. He took his time unwrapping the flat package and opened the top of a velvet box to reveal a Montblanc fountain pen engraved with his monogram. Everyone followed his movements when he sank down next to Viviana and kissed her boldly on the mouth.

"My daughter doesn't need to see that," Giles called out across the room.

Noah made a face at his cousin. "I'm certain your daughter sees more than that before you swole your wife up."

"Noah!" came a chorus from many of the women who had young children.

"Keep it clean, son," Edward warned at the same time he smothered a chuckle. He plucked another gaily wrapped gift from under the tree. "Viviana, this one is for you from your *bae*."

"What do you know about a *bae*, Dad?" Rhett called out.

Edward smiled. "I'm not so old that I don't keep up with what you young folks call one another."

Viviana was handed the small gift bag, and she removed the tissue paper and took out a square velvet box she suspected contained a piece of jewelry. An audible gasp escaped her when she saw the diamond-encrusted bangle. She handed Noah the bracelet, and he undid the double safety clasp, slipped it on her small wrist and secured it. Viviana held up her arm, and light from the overhead chandelier caught the precious stones as a hushed silence settled over the assembly.

"Well damn, brother," Rhett said under his breath. "What's next? A ring?"

Chanel landed a soft punch on Rhett's shoulder. "Stay out of it."

Viviana had bonded quickly with Noah's sister. She was lively and upbeat and had a quick laugh. Chanel admitted she'd recently joined WDG and that it would take time for her to become familiar with the company which had afforded her a privileged lifestyle. She'd admitted she hadn't had much time for romance and wanted to wait until she was secure in her career before getting involved with a man. And respecting Viviana's privacy, Chanel did not mention her relationship with her brother.

The exchange of gifts continued well past one in the morning, and when concluded, the parents gathered their sleeping children and waited for the elevator to take them to their assigned suites.

Noah caught Viviana's arm after she'd handed off Lily to Giles. "Please come with me."

"Where are we going?"

"Someplace where I can talk to you."

She followed Noah as he led her down a narrow hallway to an area outside the gourmet kitchen that doubled as the pantry. The only light came from the one in the hallway. "What do you want to talk about?"

Pulling her against his chest, he lowered his head and kissed her passionately. "I want to thank you for the pen. I'll use it whenever I have to sign off on a deal."

Leaning back, she tried to see his features in the diffused light. "Every businessman or woman should have a pen that honors their success." Going on tiptoe, she brushed a light kiss over his slightly parted lips. "And I'd like to thank you for the exquisite bracelet. I'll treasure it always."

"I had it engraved so you'll never forget me or this date."

"Why would you think I'd ever forget you?"

He angled his head. "I just hoped you wouldn't."

"There's no way I could ever forget you, Noah." She kissed him again. "Merry Christmas."

Noah nodded. "Merry Christmas, sweetheart."

Viviana eased out of his embrace and retraced her steps, leaving him staring at her back. The day had been one of discoveries. She had been introduced to the entire Wainwright clan. The exception was Brandt and his very pregnant wife, Ciara, who was expecting their first child before the end of the year. Ciara, experiencing some contractions, had decided to stay close to home and had sent her and Brandt's best wishes to everyone.

She took the staircase to the third floor and walked into the suite. Sitting on an armchair, she removed the bangle and read the inscription on the underside: *Love Always, NCW-12/25/2018*. Noah had also dated it so she could never forget when he'd given it to her. Viviana returned the bangle to the box and left it on the side table. It wasn't a piece she would wear every day but only on special occasions. And the next one was coming up in exactly one week.

It was just an hour into the new year, and the mansion was aglow with lights as formally dressed men and women whirled around the ballroom to a live band and orchestra playing tunes spanning decades. Viviana smiled up at Noah as they waltzed around the dance floor. He was breathtakingly handsome in formal dress.

The sit-down, five-course dinner had been a rousing success as guests interacted with people with whom they might have not been that familiar. The chef and his staff had outdone themselves with grilled-to-order steaks, cedar-planked fresh salmon, and crispy orange Cornish hens. The waitstaff kept wineglasses filled and were quick to see to the needs of each of the dinner guests.

Edward and Christiane, seated at the head table, thanked everyone for coming and for their generous contributions to a worthy cause and announced that everyone would be given a thank-you gift before departing.

It had taken Viviana and Christiane hours to come up with a party favor on such short notice, and they had finally decided to contact a perfumer and had ordered boxed sets of sample fragrances for men and women. Christiane was overcome with emotion once the dinner concluded and everyone had stood up and applauded.

"My mother loves you, my family loves you and I love you," Noah whispered in her ear. "And I forgot to tell you that you're the most beautiful woman here."

Viviana lowered her eyes. It had taken her a while to go through the formal gowns at her favorite boutique before she'd decided on a de rigueur, body-hugging little black dress, with a plunging neckline, wide bands crisscrossing her bared back and a generous slit from ankle to mid-thigh. Her only jewelry was a pair of diamond studs that had belonged to her maternal grandmother and Noah's bracelet.

"That's because you're biased."

"Hell yeah, I am." He spun her around and around in an intricate dance step. "What can I do to convince you to stay a little longer? You can go back with me and Giles later on in the month."

"Nothing, Noah. I've been away from home much too long lately." When she told Noah she needed to return to The Falls, he'd made arrangements for her flight and ground transportation for the following afternoon. "And because I've put out a closed-for-the-season notice, folks will begin to notice that I'm not there. Even though I've alerted the sheriff's office to check on my home, they can't watch it 24/7. Wickham Falls, like so many cities and towns in the country, has a serious opioid crisis resulting in an increase in break-ins."

"You can't say I didn't try."

"You can be very convincing, but not this time, darling. After this dance, I'm going to head upstairs and try to get some sleep. I'll see you at breakfast."

Noah nodded. "I'll take you to your room."

Viviana disarmed the security system and closed the door to the B and B. Why, she thought, did the house where she'd grown up feel so strange? That's when she realized she had been away more than she'd been there over the past month. That she had become accustomed to sharing a roof with Noah and with those he knew or was related to. Spending thirteen days in the magnificent greystone with his extended family had felt normal and natural when they'd embraced her without reservation.

To the Wainwrights, she was Noah's girlfriend, and his mother had dropped hints that she wouldn't mind having her as a daughter-in-law because she also wanted another girl. Viviana did not want to disappoint the woman by informing her that her relationship with her son was too new to talk about an engagement, marriage and grandchildren.

She left her luggage by the door and went about the task of opening windows to let in fresh air. After showering and changing into sweats, she planned to drive to the supermarket to restock the fridge and prepare dinner. Dusting and vacuuming all of the rooms and guesthouses would have to wait for another day.

Viviana had been back in The Falls for almost two weeks when the doorbell rang, and when she opened the door it was to see someone she'd never wanted to come face-to-face with again.

"What the hell do you want?"

"May I come in?"

"No, you may not." She'd caught glimpses of Myles Duncan from afar, but this was the first time she'd seen him close-up, and time had not been particularly kind to him. He'd gained weight, his hair was thinning and his short beard failed to hide his pockmarked cheeks. His dark brown eyes brimmed with anger.

"I came to tell you that I've decided to reverse my vote to approve your application even though I don't like being blackmailed."

"What! Why?"

"Please don't play the innocent, Viviana. Your rich boyfriend threatened to expose an incident that was expunged from my record when I was a college student. I was accused of assaulting a girl at a frat party, and because she was drunk and couldn't remember all that had happened, I was charged with underage drinking and expelled from the fraternity, and if I completed two hundred hours of community service, my record would be wiped clean. I suppose if you have enough money, you can get people to roll over on their mothers."

Viviana felt as if her heart was beating outside of her chest. "I don't know what you're talking about. Noah wouldn't blackmail you."

A sardonic smile twisted Myles's mouth. "It's apparent you don't know him. Your application has been approved, and when you come to the hearing next week, the chairperson will give you the letter attesting to this.

And let your gangster boyfriend know we've also approved his application to build."

Viviana stood there, numbly staring at the taillights of Myles's car as he drove away. Her hands were shaking uncontrollably as she attempted to close the door. If what Myles had told her was true, then she knew her relationship would change. She remembered Noah saying to her, "Don't worry, sweetheart. We'll figure out something."

She was very calm when she tapped his number into her phone. "Hey sweetheart. What's up?" Noah asked when answering her call.

"I need to talk to you about something."

"Talk to me, babe."

"I received word that our permits have been approved."

"That's wonderful news."

"Is it?" she asked him.

"Of course it is, Viv."

"No, it's not when you resort to blackmail."

There came a beat. "What the hell are you talking about?"

Viviana repeated everything Myles told her.

"You're wrong, Viviana. I had nothing to do with blackmailing him into changing his vote."

"Someone did, Noah. So, you better check out your people up there and get to the bottom of this. I don't intend to repeat the underhanded tactics that my ancestors did to get ahead. I have to live here and you don't, so right now I don't want to have anything to do with you. We're done!" She ended the call and threw the cell phone across the room. It hit the wall and landed on a chair.

Viviana wanted to cry but couldn't. She wanted to scream, but her voice was locked in her throat. Not again, she thought. Just when she'd believed she had hit the mother lode with a man she could trust, he'd become like a snake shedding its skin, leaving the scaly object behind when he slithered away.

Walking into the parlor, she opened a bottle of port and poured a generous amount into a rock glass. She sat down and sipped the sweet liquid until she felt the tension leave her body. Then she curled up on the love seat, closed her eyes and cried. When tears no longer flowed, she promised herself it would be the last time she'd ever cry over a man.

"He's on the phone and doesn't want to be disturbed."

Noah glared at his father's administrative assistant and pushed open the door to the CEO's private office. "Put down the phone, Dad."

Edward held up a hand. "Wait a minute, son."

Reaching over, Noah took the receiver from Edward's hand and placed it in the console. "This can't wait."

Rage suffused the older man's face. "Have you gone and lost your mind? That was someone willing to sell us several buildings in a gentrified Brooklyn neighborhood."

Resting his hands on the antique mahogany desk, Noah leaned close enough to feel Edward's breath on his face. "What the hell did you do?"

"What the hell are you talking about?" Edward asked.

"Did you get someone to blackmail Myles Duncan into reversing his vote?"

Edward crossed his arms over his crisp white shirt in a gesture Noah interpreted as protective and hostile at the same time. "I gave Duncan's name to Kennedy, and he found out a lot of things about your girlfriend's admirer. It appears Duncan had slept with a number of girls who'd had too much to drink, and couldn't remember what he'd done to them."

"So, you used the man's sexual proclivities to blackmail him into changing his vote."

Edward slowly shook his head. "You came to me with a problem, and I solved it for you. You're a businessman, Noah, not a choirboy. And when it comes to business, there are times when you not only have to get your hands a little dirty but you also have to fight dirty. And I learned from one of the best street fighters I've ever known—Wyatt Wainwright. He built this empire to afford you and everyone that's a Wainwright a privileged lifestyle other people can only fantasize about.

"Do you think you'd be able ride around in a car with a six-figure sticker price, or fly in private jets, or give Viviana a bracelet that cost more than some working-class stiff makes in two years if I hadn't done things I had to do to seal a deal? No, son. So, don't come in here with your holier-than-thou airs. Grow the hell up, or get out of the game."

"That's exactly what I intend to do, Father. I'm out. And I'll stay out until you apologize to Viviana for what you've done. Now I know why Jordan wants nothing to do with WDG, and if you continue to emulate your father, you're going to lose all of your children. You have a good day."

Turning on his heel, he walked out and took the elevator down to the street. He pulled up the collar of his topcoat as he signaled for an approaching taxi. He didn't want to go home, so he told the cabbie to just drive and he'd tell him when he wanted him to stop. He called Jordan's office, and the receptionist told him Mr. Wainwright was in court and that he could leave a message. Noah told her it was okay and that he would reach him later at home.

Leaning forward, he tapped on the Plexiglas partition and gave the driver the address to the greystone on Fifth Avenue. Once he arrived, it took Noah less than an hour to pack his bag with enough clothes to last a week, and then he called a car service to take him to the airport where he purchased a first-class ticket to Charleston, West Virginia. He had a two-hour wait for the next flight out of New York with a connecting one in DC. He was leaving New York without saying goodbye to his mother or sister. He would leave it to Edward to explain his unexpected departure.

It was close to nine thirty when the taxi pulled up in front of the Wickham Falls Bed and Breakfast. There was a light on the first floor and several in upstairs bedrooms. He paid the driver and walked to the front door to face the most difficult test of his life.

Noah rang the bell and waited for Viviana to answer it. He rang it over and over until the door finally opened and he saw firsthand what she had gone through. Her eyes were swollen, and he knew she had been crying.

"May I come in?"

She blinked slowly. "Did you come to get your car?"

"No, Viviana. I came to explain everything."

Her eyes narrowed. "There's nothing to explain."

"Yes, there is. Now, please let me in or I'll yell so loud your nearest neighbor will hear everything I have to say to you."

She opened the door wider. "Come in, but you can't stay."

Noah dropped his bag and scooped her up in his arms, ignoring the blows raining down on his back and shoulders. He carried her into the parlor, sat on the love seat and settled her over his lap. "I want you to listen to what I have to say, and if you want me to leave, I will. But if I walk out that door, I'm never coming back. And our deal is null and void with no strings attached."

Viviana didn't move, not even her eyes, when Noah disclosed the confrontation between him and his father earlier that morning. She didn't want to believe he had walked away from everything he'd worked for because Edward had believed he was doing the right thing not only for Noah but also for her.

"Are you really through with WDG?"

"Yes. The only way I'll consider going back is if my father calls you and apologizes, and makes a promise never to blackmail anyone again And I'm going to insist the details of every deal be outlined during board meetings or I'm out. If not, then I'll apply for a position with an architectural firm in Philly or DC.

Once Edward said what he did, it reminded me of you when you talk about the Wolfes who took advantage of their workers by any means necessary to increase their wealth and power. I don't want you to think I'm like them, Viv."

"But your family is?" she argued softly.

"Think about what you're saying. You're judging me the same way folks here judge you. I'm only responsible for what I do and not what my family does. I'm going to pick up my car and check into a hotel up on the interstate. You have my number, so call me whenever my father contacts you. And if he doesn't, then this is goodbye. And remember, I'll always love you."

Viviana watched him walk out, and something wouldn't permit her to go after him. Maybe, she thought, it was better this way. No histrionics.

Viviana sat on the window seat in her bedroom watching rivulets of rain slide down the windows. It had been raining steadily for three days, and her mood matched the weather. It was more than six weeks since Noah had walked out of the house and her life. Mya had called, inviting her to come over, but she had used so many excuses that she struggled to come up with another. She didn't want Giles's wife to ask her about Noah because she didn't want to bring the woman into something about which she might not have knowledge. Every family had its secrets, and Giles might not have made his wife privy to those closely held secrets.

She knew she had to get up and prepare something to eat, but all she wanted to do was crawl back into bed and pull the covers up over her head, just as she'd done as a child when she'd heard her mother pleading with her father to go get help. Viviana hadn't known the kind of help he needed, but apparently it was very important to Annette because whenever he walked out, she would cry inconsolably.

Get it together, girl. Remember, you're a survivor. Her inner voice was talking to her again, and she slipped off the window seat and went downstairs to the kitchen to fix what she thought of as comfort food: chili. She picked up a can of kidney beans from a shelf in the pantry when the doorbell chimed throughout the first floor. The B and B was still closed, and she wondered who was at the door.

She peered through a curtain to find the figure of a tall man. There was something about him that looked familiar, and then she recognized him when he looked back her. Edward Wainwright hadn't called her but had come to see her. She unlocked the door and saw lines of strain extending from his nose to his mouth.

He smiled, but it looked more like a grimace. "May I come in?"

"Yes. Please." Even though she wanted to hate the man for what he had done to her and Noah, she couldn't.

Edward wiped his feet on the thick mat and then set down his leather carry-on. "I was wondering if the B and B is open, and if you have an available room for the night."

Viviana didn't know whether to laugh or order the man off her property. She decided on the former. "Yes,

I do happen to have an available room. Please come with me, and I'll show you."

"After I change, I think we need to talk."

She glanced at him over her shoulder. "What about, Edward?"

"About my sins. About how I did something, despite knowing how Noah feels about anything that's immoral. Of all of my children, he's the one with the most integrity, and I failed him."

"I was just about to put up a pot of chili, and if you want some, then I'll make enough for the two of us."

The sparkle was back in the blue eyes when he smiled. "That's good."

Over bowls of chili with ground beef and topped with diced onions and shredded pepper-jack cheese, Edward disclosed everything that had transpired, from the time Noah had told him about failing to get the permits to turning the matter over to the company's investigator. "If I'd believed it would lead to me losing my son and him losing you, I never would've done it."

Reaching across the table, Viviana patted the back of his heavily veined hand. "We all make mistakes, Edward. It's only when we don't acknowledge them that we're burdened with guilt."

"Do you forgive me for what I've done?"

She nodded, smiling. "When I opened the door and saw you standing there, I forgave you because I knew it must have taken a lot of courage for you to come down here to see me. Now, why don't you go upstairs and go to sleep. You look tired."

"I'm more than tired, child. I'm exhausted." He flashed a sad smile. "Now I know why Noah fell in love with you. You have a forgiving heart. And you're a hell of a cook."

"Good night, Edward."

She watched him walk out of the kitchen. Pushing to her feet, she picked up her cell phone and tapped Noah's number. He picked up on the first ring.

"I know."

"What do you know?" she asked.

"I know that Edward was coming to see you."

"How did you know?"

"My mother called and told me. When she found out what he'd done, she called her lawyer and told him to draw up divorce papers. She told him it was the last time she was going to let him mess with her kids. I suppose Dad got the message and he told her he was coming to see you."

"Where are you, Noah?"

"I've been staying with Giles and Mya."

"You mean to tell me you've been in The Falls all this time?"

"Yeah. Mya has been trying to get you to come over, but you wouldn't bite."

"That's because I didn't want to involve her in our mess."

"Mya knows the whole sordid story about the Wainwrights, so you don't have to concern yourself about telling tales out of school."

"When am I going to see you?"

"I'm going to stay here until Giles comes back from

the Bahamas. Then you'll need to get a suite ready because when I move in, I'm not moving out."

Her smile was dazzling. "And I don't want you to move out. Your Dad is upstairs sleeping in one of the suites for guests. I'm going to try to convince him to hang out here for a few days so he gets a little country."

"It's going to take a lot to get the city out of Edward, but if anybody can get him to change, then you can."

"He says he likes my cooking."

"I like your cooking, your sexy mouth and your—"

"Don't you dare say it on an open line. I'll be here whenever Giles gets back."

"Viv?"

"What, Noah?"

"I love you to death."

"That goes double for me."

Epilogue

A year later...

Viviana looped her arm over Noah's shoulder as she posed for photos for those who'd come to their engagement party. The brilliant spring sun fired the large diamond on her left hand. Every room in the B and B and the two guesthouses were filled with Wainwrights. And Giles and Mya had opened their own home to accommodate the overflow.

Christiane had wanted to host the party at the Fifth Avenue mansion, but Viviana had insisted they come to The Falls to see what it was about the town that now counted two Wainwrights among their citizenry.

Leland and Angela had driven up with the twins from North Carolina, and her father had come down from Philadelphia to help her celebrate one of the happiest days of her life—thus far. She and Noah had planned to marry Christmas Day on Emerald Cove, and both sides of the family were expected to attend.

She smiled up at her fiancé, looking dapper in his suit jacket. "I love you," she whispered for his ears only.

He winked at her. "Love you more."

"Look this way," a woman's voice called out, and Viviana turned her head to smile at her future sister-in-law who snapped their picture. A smile parted her lips when she saw her brother laughing at something Emory had said.

At that moment she knew nothing was more important than family, and when she married Noah, the Remingtons would become part of a large extended family and afforded the same privileges as the Wainwrights. And when she exchanged vows with Noah, it would become the sweetest deal they would ever seal.

* * * * *

Look for the next Wickham Falls Weddings book in September 2019!

And be sure to check out these other great stories by Rochelle Alers:

Twins for the Soldier
The Sheriff of Wickham Falls
Her Wickham Falls SEAL
Claiming the Captain's Baby

Available now from Harlequin Special Edition!

Get 4 FREE REWARDS!

We'll send you 2 FREE Books plus 2 FREE Mystery Gifts.

Harlequin® Special Edition books feature heroines finding the balance between their work life and personal life on the way to finding true love.

FREE
Value Over
$20

SPECIAL EXCERPT FROM

H HARLEQUIN®

TM

SPECIAL EDITION

*Losing Miranda broke Matt Grimes's heart.
And kept him from the knowledge of his pending
fatherhood. Now Miranda Contreras has returned
to Rocking Chair, Texas—with their eight-year-old
daughter. Matt should be angry! What other secrets
could Miranda be keeping? But all he sees is a chance
to be the family they were meant to be.*

Read on for a sneak preview of
The Cowboy's Secret Family,
the next great book in USA TODAY *bestselling author
Judy Duarte's Rocking Chair Rodeo miniseries.*

When Matt looked up, she offered him a shy smile. "Like I said, I'm sorry. I should have told you that you were a father."

"You've got that right."

"I've made mistakes, but Emily isn't one of them. She's a great kid. So for now, let's focus on her."

"All right." Matt uncrossed his arms and raked a hand through his hair. "But just for the record, I would've done anything in my power to take care of you and Emily."

"I know." And that was why she'd walked away from him. Matt would have stood up to her father, challenged his threat, only to be knocked to his knees—and worse.

No, leaving town and cutting all ties with Matt was the only thing she could've done to protect him.

As she stood in the room where their daughter was conceived, as she studied the only man she'd ever loved, the memories crept up on her…the old feelings, too.

When she was sixteen, there'd been something about the fun-loving nineteen-year-old cowboy that had drawn her attention. And whatever it was continued to tug at her now. But she shook it off. Too many years had passed; too many tears had been shed.

Besides, an unwed single mother who was expecting another man's baby wouldn't stand a chance with a champion bull rider who had his choice of pretty cowgirls. And she'd best not forget that.

"Aw, hell," Matt said, as he ran a hand through his hair again and blew out a weary sigh. "Maybe you did Emily a favor by leaving when you did. Who knows what kind of father I would have made back then. Or even now."

Don't miss
The Cowboy's Secret Family *by Judy Duarte,*
available June 2019 wherever
Harlequin® Special Edition books and ebooks are sold.

www.Harlequin.com

Looking for more satisfying love stories
with community and family at their core?

Check out **Harlequin®** **Special Edition**
and **Love Inspired®** books!

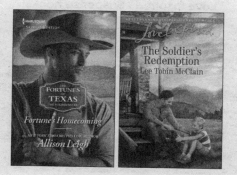

New books available every month!

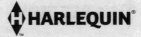

Love Harlequin romance?

DISCOVER.

Be the first to find out about promotions,
news and exclusive content!

 Facebook.com/HarlequinBooks

 Twitter.com/HarlequinBooks

Instagram.com/HarlequinBooks

Pinterest.com/HarlequinBooks

ReaderService.com

EXPLORE.

Sign up for the Harlequin e-newsletter and
download a free book from any series at
TryHarlequin.com.

CONNECT.

Join our Harlequin community to share
your thoughts and connect with other
romance readers!
Facebook.com/groups/HarlequinConnection

 **HARLEQUIN**®

**ROMANCE WHEN
YOU NEED IT**

HSOCIAL2018

Reward the book lover in you!

Earn points on your purchase of new Harlequin books from participating retailers.

Turn your points into **FREE BOOKS** of your choice!

Join for FREE today at **www.HarlequinMyRewards.com.**

Harlequin My Rewards is a free program (no fees) without any commitments or obligations.

MYR18